WHEN THE CAMERAS STOP ROLLING...

BY
CONNIE COX

MILLS & BOON

First published in Great Britain 2013
by Mills & Boon, an imprint of Harlequin (UK) Limited.
Harlequin (UK) Limited, Eton House,
18-24 Paradise Road, Richmond, Surrey TW9 1SR

© Connie Cox 2013

ISBN: 978 0 263 89899 6

Harlequin (UK) policy is to use papers that are natural, renewable and recyclable products and made from wood grown in sustainable forests. The logging and manufacturing process conform to the legal environmental regulations of the country of origin.

Printed and bound in Spain
by Blackprint CPI, Barcelona

'ine. I'll go."

Mark narrowed his gaze at her. "I don't need a pity date."

"That's good, since I don't do pity dates. I only pepperoni, extra onions."

"Extra onions? You don't do goodnight kisses, either, then, do you?"

"Never on a first date to a pizza parlor."

"Is it the venue? You need a more upscale wine-and-dinery?"

"Nope. It's the first date thing. Why waste a good kiss if I'm not sure about a second date yet?"

"Right. Because kisses are in limited supply."

She cocked an eyebrow at him. "Mine are rare, which makes them extremely valuable."

"Then I'll treasure it properly should I ever decide to accept one."

"*Should* you decide?" She gave him her best smoldering look, along with a very deliberate lip-lick. "I could make you beg."

"I'd like to see you try."

His answer was flippant, but the widening of pupils told another story. Eva would bet anything his pulse was racing.

At least she wasn't lusting alone. She found herself lean
sucked tow

Dear Reader,

Have you ever met a man who makes your heart race, your nerves tingle and your world a more exciting place to wake up to?

From the moment Dr Eva Veracruz saw Dr Mark O'Donnell swagger across her talk show studio and flash his smile at her cameras, she knew he would be trouble. And she'd had enough trouble in her life to know better than to go looking for more.

But her only choice was to smile for the camera. After all, the show must go on.

Experience had taught Mark O'Donnell that smart and sexy meant trouble. Instincts told him Eva Veracruz was trouble with a capital T. But instincts were overruled by the way Eva's deep dark eyes sparkled under the bright lights.

The chemistry they share in front of an audience doesn't stop when the lights go down. In fact, that chemistry turns to an offscreen passion that Eva and Mark keep from acting upon.

But real life isn't scripted with witty sound bites and perfect people who solve their dilemmas between commercial breaks.

When their life stories have more conflict than the most dramatic of stage plays, can their made-for-TV romance survive?

What really happens when the cameras stop rolling?

Connie Cox

Connie would love to hear from you. Visit her website at www.ConnieCox.com

Connie Cox has loved Harlequin Mills & Boon® romances since she was a young teen. To be a Harlequin Mills & Boon® author now is a fantasy come to life. By training, Connie is an electrical engineer. Through her first job, working on nuclear scanners and other medical equipment, she had a unique perspective on the medical world. She is fascinated by the inner strength of medical professionals, who must balance emotional compassion with stoic logic, and is honoured to showcase the passion of these dedicated professionals through her own passion of writing. Married to the boy-next-door, Connie is the proud mother of one terrific daughter and son-in-law and one precocious dachshund.

Recent titles by Connie Cox:

HIS HIDDEN AMERICAN BEAUTY
THE BABY WHO SAVED DR CYNICAL
RETURN OF THE REBEL SURGEON

**Available in eBook format
from www.millsandboon.co.uk**

CHAPTER ONE

Dr. Eva Veracruz glanced at the clock for the fifth time in as many seconds.

The buzz from the live studio audience for *Ask the Doc* was upbeat. A good sign.

The guest speaker was not yet in the studio. A bad sign. A very bad sign.

"Where is he, Phil? Where's this supermodel doctor you found who's supposed to catapult our ratings past our competitor?"

Her producer, Phil, shrugged. "He'll be here."

"Our viewers trust us to give them good medical information and I respect that trust. I thought you did, too. I'd much rather have an accomplished speaker who knows our topic, regardless of looks."

"If we don't get our ratings up during sweeps week, our viewers won't get any information, good, bad or otherwise."

Ask the Doc might only be a local television show, but local in the New Orleans area translated to quite a large viewing audience.

Eva had heard rumors of syndication, rumors she wholeheartedly supported. Bigger and better, right?

That had been before their competitor station had decided to run a reality show against their time slot. Eating bugs and getting knocked into the water by giant blow-up fists was trumping good, solid medical advice.

Their sponsors were not happy. How could they sell their balm to cure the diaper rash of their viewers' babies if no one was watching their commercials?

If they couldn't beat the national reality show they would never get a chance to become syndicated as they would be off the air instead.

Phil lifted an eyebrow. "I know my job. I checked his background. Dr. O'Donnell is a respected E.R. doctor who has become renowned for recognizing heart attacks in women."

"But can he talk on television?"

"Getting him to talk is *your* job."

Since she hadn't gotten to meet him yet, she had no idea what kind of speaking talent this Dr. O'Donnell had. But she *was* good at her job.

Phil looked at the clock. It was time. "Stall and watch the wings."

"Got it." The intro music played as she walked onto the set, thinking fast and revising her opening speech in her head. She would normally tell her audience about her guest, but if he didn't show...

Eva waved to the crowd, catching a glimpse of herself in the monitors. Her jet-black curls were going wild down her back and around her face as the humidity of the New Orleans morning crept into the television studio.

The make-up artist had gone big and bold with the red lipstick to complement her scarlet dress—as if her big mouth needed any more help. Even without cosmetics her lips already looked like they had been overfilled with collagen, even though she'd never touched the stuff.

She did have to admit that her olive complexion looked a lot warmer with the hint of red showing from beneath her white lab coat.

"Hello, New Orleans. Welcome to *Ask the Doc.* I'm your host, Dr. Eva Veracruz. We have a very important show today for all you hard-working women out there. We'll be talking about heart attacks and the signs and symptoms we all need to be aware of."

From the corner of her eye, she saw Phil give her the thumbs-up as he pointed to a shadowy figure in the wings.

Eva revised her opening remarks on the fly. "And we have a guest who has first-hand knowledge of our topic today. Let's give a big hand to Dr. Mark O'Donnell from the Crescent Street Emergency Care Clinic."

The crowd's polite applause audibly increased as Dr. O'Donnell came into view. Phil, the show's producer, had accomplished his goal. The man could have been an underwear model.

At least six feet four to her five feet eleven plus four-inch heels, he was taller than her. His eyes were a vivid Aegean green that could only come from tinted contacts. His haircut looked vaguely rebellious, like it had been close cropped once upon a time and now needed a touch-up. It was a cross between brown and a very dark russet.

He was not the type she usually went for, preferring a more military look. But, then, she'd had no type in quite a while, which might explain her extreme reaction.

Not only did he make her pulse throb, her whole metabolism seemed to pick up speed as he came toward her. What was it about him that made her adrenaline rush?

It wasn't just his looks. It was his attitude.

She was a sucker for a strong personality. Since she knew that about herself, she also knew to keep him at arm's length. Not a problem. She wasn't ready for a man in her life. She was still recovering from the last one.

The show's intro song faded into the pre-taped segment she'd recorded yesterday with information on how to contact local emergency care personnel and where to write in for heart-attack information while she got the good doctor seated.

His swagger made the audience sit up and take notice even if he didn't deign to look at them. He walked in like he owned the place.

He had the kind of cocky attitude she would never fall for again.

She could tell by the clothes he wore that he was a rule breaker, which too easily transitioned into heartbreaker for any woman foolish enough to get close to him.

The show requested business attire, in his case a suit and tie. Instead, he wore his lab coat over scrubs.

With the way the lighting was set, the white of his coat with the white of her own custom-tailored lab coat would blanch the set.

She could see her producer already scrambling behind the cameras, trying to figure out how to salvage the video quality. How could she help from her hosting chair?

At her gesture, Dr. O'Donnell stood in front of the chair opposite her.

"Please say something so the sound engineer can do a final microphone check," she requested.

He looked at a loss, then said, "Something."

Eva couldn't help smirking. This was going to be a challenging show.

Dr. O'Donnell would do his guest shot. She'd make him look like a natural in front of the camera by feeding him the answers to the questions she asked him and covering his pauses with insightful comments. Their ratings would soar and he would be another featured rerun during their off season.

Had it only been two years since she'd left the free clinic environment and entered the television market? She'd learned so much since then. Her innate ambition nagged at her, making her anxious to move up to the next level—national exposure. Her agent had said it was time to put the word out on the street that she was interested in bigger and better things before everyone heard about *Ask the Doc's* falling ratings.

But, then, committing to her television career would mean she'd made a clear-cut decision to leave the practice of medicine behind.

Good, right? She would no longer be plagued by nebulous thoughts of one day returning to clinical work as she trod her newly chosen path of being a television personality.

Could she find fulfillment, could she find peace if she never called herself a doctor again?

Her mind skittered past the possibility of turning her back on the career she'd spent her whole life working toward.

Concentrate on now. Not the future, Eva. Interviewing the pretty-boy doctor who had a blank expression on his sculpted face took precedence over everything else. She could salvage this interview. She was a professional.

"Welcome, Dr. O'Donnell." She made a split-second decision. Instead of offering her hand to shake, she unbuttoned her own lab coat and whipped it off. Speaking to the cameras, she waved her hand down the length of her wrap-front dress.

"Notice the red dress I'm wearing today in support of educating everyone about the signs of heart attack in women."

She ignored the self-consciousness she felt that the dress was intentionally a smidgeon too tight to fit better under her lab coat.

"Whenever you see a red dress, refresh your memory on the early symptoms of a heart attack. Your early response could save a loved one's life. Isn't that right, Dr. O'Donnell?"

She stared into his deep blue-green eyes, noticing the amber ring around his pupils.

He stared back.

Finally, he answered, "Yes."

A single, monotone response. This was going to be one of *those* interviews.

Pretty is as pretty does. Eva would gladly trade this eye candy before her for a glib, knowledgeable doctor of any physical description.

Well, if she was going to have to muscle through this, she might as well get something out of it.

Unapologetically, she would enjoy the view while he was here.

She waved him into the visitor's chair, noticing he hesitated before she seated herself. Good manners? Or a suspicious nature, not agreeing to anything until he'd made up his mind?

For all Eva's training and experience in the nuances of body language, she couldn't be sure but highly suspected the latter.

Very aware of the tightness of her dress without her lab coat to cover it, she positioned herself so the camera wouldn't stare straight down her cleavage—which meant Dr. O'Donnell would have to.

This set wasn't designed for keeping a comfortable amount of personal space between the host and the guest. Instead, it was laid out to give the appearance of intimacy, hopefully translating into trust and confidence for the viewer.

"Welcome to *Ask the Doc*, Dr. O'Donnell. Tell me, how many cases of heart attack in women do you see compared to men?"

She left her question broad, knowing she could work with any answer he gave her. That's what her producers attributed to the show's success, her ability to think fast.

She wished they'd take into consideration the three and a half years she'd spent at the busiest drug-abuse treatment clinic in New Orleans, working with walk-in patients. Talk about having to think fast on your feet...

So far, the producers had sidestepped her suggestion for a

hard-hitting drug-abuse segment, but Eva planned to insist, when her contract renegotiations came due, that a series on drug abuse be included that ranged from family recognition and prevention to consequences, treatment options and success rates for battling addiction.

Too many people needed this information just like too many people shied away from it.

Though, right now, she had a more immediate problem as Dr. O'Donnell shied away from the camera.

After the night he'd had, Mark fought off his exhausted stupor. Searching for a boost of energy, he looked at the woman across from him, all hair and boobs and luscious lips ripe for—

"Do you see many women coming into the E.R. knowing they're having a heart attack?"

This was her second question and he hadn't even answered the first one yet.

Come on, O'Donnell. Get your head in the game.

"We don't see as many women come in with suspected heart attacks as men, but that's not to say women don't have as many heart attacks. All these years while we've been thinking men are the majority of heart-attack victims, we haven't been diagnosing women properly."

His host nodded encouragingly, as if she were coaxing answers from a child. "In fact, heart disease is the number-one killer in women, isn't it, Dr. O'Donnell?"

"Yes, it is." Mark thought of the woman he'd admitted last night. He'd insisted the lab run an EKG even though she'd thought she had flu.

"Tell us some of the symptoms as we post them on our viewers' screens." Dr. Veracruz pointed, not so subtly, to the monitor.

Even in his mind, Mark stumbled over calling her a doctor. She was no more a medical doctor than he was a ballerina.

What was her name? Edna? Ella? Eva.

She looked like an Eva, every overstated voluptuous inch of her.

Maybe, just maybe, she had her doctorate in journalism or television. Could a person get a degree in talk-show hosting?

But this woman with her long, dangling earrings and cleavage deeper than the Grand Canyon would probably faint at the sight of blood.

Mark read the first bullet point. Shortness of breath.

He looked into the lens like the public relations specialists in his university's athletic department had trained him to do during his football years and flashed the camera's blinking red light a smile.

"Here are the top signs of having a heart attack."

Mark ignored Eva's raised eyebrows.

"If you feel like you've run a marathon and haven't taken a single step, or if you can't draw in a deep breath, go to the emergency room. You might be having a heart attack."

His quirky tone drew a small laugh from the audience. Laughter meant they were listening and listening meant they were learning.

And education was the only reason he'd agreed to be on this show to start with. His own beloved grandmother had died of a heart attack. If only she'd known, if only those around her had known, maybe she would still be here for him and for his sister.

She had been their only reality in the world of fakeness for appearances' sake where his socialite parents had insisted they all live.

The audience waited for the next sign on the list. Mark reached for the sense of humor most people thought was too quirky.

"If you feel weak in the knees and your world is spinning around you and you're not about to walk down the aisle and say 'I do', go to the emergency room. You might be having a heart attack."

From the corner of his eye, he saw Dr. Veracruz sit back in her chair, obviously giving him the spotlight.

Mark had to do some quick thinking to phrase the other symptoms the same way.

"If you feel nauseous and it's not from overindulgence in the French Quarter, go to the emergency room. You might be having a heart attack.

"If you feel upper abdominal indigestion, don't even try to blame it on that spicy Creole dish your sister-in-law made, go to the emergency room. You might be having a heart attack."

He paused, going blank as the remaining symptoms blinked on the monitors.

Dr. Veracruz gave him a quick glance then sat forward, giving a subtle off-camera sign to the camera operator, who pulled back to get both of them in the shot.

Smiling, she said, "If your back muscles are in spasm, as if you've spent all night dancing the tango and you haven't even lifted a teacup, go to the emergency room. You might be having a heart attack."

She gave him a conspiratorial look, as if they'd planned this out ahead of time as she finished off the list.

"And the classic symptom. If you feel like an elephant is sitting on your chest, go to the emergency room. You might be having a heart attack."

Mark nodded toward her, silently telling her he'd take it from there. "At the first signs of a heart attack, chew an aspirin. Crush it with your teeth as you may not be able to swallow it."

Dr. Veracruz dovetailed with her own comment. "And after you take that aspirin, go to the hospital. Because…"

She pointed to the audience, who all called out in sync, "You might be having a heart attack."

Mark steepled his hands and gave the camera a dead-serious stare, wanting to make his point as strongly as he could. "The second biggest problem with women having heart attacks is that they don't want to bother anyone just because they're not feeling well. Take a lesson from the boys, ladies. You're important enough to bother people. Even if it's a false alarm, you're worth the bother. Your family would rather have you alive and embarrassed about a bit of gas than dead because you tried to not be a bother. So, at the first signs of a heart attack, go immediately to the emergency room."

Eva gave the camera an equally serious stare. "And remember. Don't drive yourself. If you do, you'll put everyone on the road in danger. Call for emergency transport. Right, Dr. O'Donnell?"

"Right," he said on cue. No one would ever accuse him of not being a team player.

Eva gave Mark an affirmative nod of her head. "And now a word from our sponsor."

As they cut the microphones, Eva looked over at her guest with a very revised opinion of him.

"Nice job. We didn't have a chance to introduce ourselves." Not able to resist the jibe about his lateness, she held out her hand. "Eva Veracruz."

"Mark. Sorry to be late. I had an emergency right before I left."

"Since you work in E.R., I'm thinking that's a typical job hazard, right?"

"Yes, it is." He put a hand on the leg of his scrubs. "This time it required a wardrobe change. That's a suit I'll never wear again. I didn't think you'd want me showing up wearing blood and guts."

"You're right. Scrubs are a better choice." Again, she had

to revise her opinion of him upwards. If he kept this up, she might actually end up liking him. "We have a short question-and-answer session with the audience and then we're done. Maybe we could—"

Before she could set up a coffee date he cut her off. "How can you answer medical questions without being a real doctor?"

"Not a real doctor? What do you mean?" But Eva knew what he meant. She'd heard it from too many people before.

She didn't look like most people's typical stereotype of a doctor and the studio make-up and hair department didn't help, playing up her sexuality for the ratings.

But, then, why should she have to de-emphasize her femininity? Wasn't it about time for women to stop having to prove they could have both brains and bosoms?

Her producer waved his hand for her attention. "Live in…" He made finger motions for five, four, three, two and then pointed at her.

Gesturing for Mark to stand, she did the same, self-conscious that the skirt of her clingy dress could use a straightening tug where it had crept up her legs. Usually, her lab coat covered problems like that. But adjusting her skirt length now would only draw attention to the problem.

Microphone in hand, she said to the camera, "*Ask the Doc* is back and ready for our live audience's questions. If you would like to be a member of our audience, send an email to the address now on your screen. We'd love to answer your questions in person, too."

This was the tricky part of the show and required great time management from her.

The producers saved it to the end so they could adjust the time if the guest speakers went long—which they had with Mark's inventive way of presenting heart attack symptoms. But he'd made a dry list of symptoms memorable and that's all that counted for such a frightening and deadly medical emergency. The audience would be wildly receptive to him and have many questions for such an approachable man.

But there was always at least one, often more than one, in the audience who got too personal for public television. That same person usually rambled, hanging on to the spotlight as long as possible. Eva's job was to divert them while seeming sympathetic. Some days this worked better than others.

This was the only part about her job she would avoid if she could.

She walked toward the audience, feeling Mark right behind her, obviously not needing her cue to move center stage. "Now, who has questions?"

The first hand up was from a staff member the producer had planted in the audience. He set the tone of intelligent yet brief questions. Eva wasn't too thrilled about her producer's subterfuge, but show management wasn't her job, as they often reminded her. She was the expert—the talking head— not the boss. And her paycheck paid many bills, including her grandmother's nursing-home supplements and her huge student-loan debts.

A frazzled woman in the third row began jumping up and down in her seat with that certain body language that said, I'm here to tell you my whole life's medical history on television and I dare you to try and stop me. Eva took care to avoid eye contact.

Looking past the woman's raised and waving hand, she pointed to her undercover staff assistant.

But before she could reach the assistant with the microphone, Mark thrust his own microphone into the jumping woman's face.

He put his arm around her shoulders to still her fidgeting as the camera moved in close. "How can I help you today?"

Eva thought the woman would swoon right then and there.

All they needed was someone to faint on set to lose those sponsors who were hanging in there for them.

Instead, the woman grabbed the microphone and held it close to her mouth to speak into it.

From the corner of her eye Eva saw the alarm on her sound engineer's face as he shoved slide knobs to lower the volume before the woman's voice blasted everyone's television speakers into mush.

But Mark purposely covered the woman's hand and pulled the microphone away to the proper distance.

Eva was beginning to suspect he'd done this kind of work before.

The woman cleared her throat. She was now red in the face. "Ever since I was a little girl…" She stopped talking as she teared up.

Mark patted her on the shoulder. "Deep breath."

The woman gave him a watery smile. "When I get excited, I can feel my heart try to beat out of my chest, then it just seems to stop and I feel dizzy."

Mark raised his eyebrows as he wrapped his arm more securely around her. "Are you feeling that way now? Have you ever passed out?"

"Once or twice."

"Please, have a seat." Mark helped her into her chair and whipped out his stethoscope. With a shiny white smile, Mark asked, "May I listen to your heart?"

Starry-eyed, the woman nodded.

The man had charisma, no doubt about it. But that bit about her not being a real doctor still stung. Being pretty— or in his case extraordinarily handsome—couldn't make up for being mean.

As Mark took the time to listen to the woman's heart, the producer instructed a camera to zoom in on Eva, expecting her to fill in the dead air space. So much for thinking Mark had live studio experience.

To the camera, she said, "When a doctor listens to your heart, she is listening for several things, including a steady rhythm."

Of course, everyone in the world already knew that, but at this point in the show Eva would spout anything that came to mind to keep the action moving along. With Mark doing personal examinations in her public forum, her only hope of making this part of the show work was to avoid a silent studio. Any intelligent information she could pass on to her audience was a bonus.

Wrestling control of her show away from her guest, she looked out towards the crowd. "While Dr. O'Donnell is performing his examination, does anyone else have questions?"

Without being called on, a young man in front of her stood up. "My son has recently developed the same symptoms as that woman. His doctor has diagnosed a congenital heart murmur and is requiring a series of tests before he'll sign off for my son to play football. He's played sports all his life. To tell you the truth, playing sports is the only thing that keeps him interested in school. How can I tell a high-energy teenager he can't play a sport he loves when he's never had any problems before?"

It was one of *those* questions, the kind that had no happy answer. She knew, first hand, how hard it was to keep some teenagers in school. Eva hid her sigh.

Mark startled her by answering from across the studio. "Playing sports with a congenital medical condition, particularly a heart murmur, is a topic that is under fierce discussion in the medical community. Many of us doctors know the value of sports in our children's development. Make sure you have a doctor who will do whatever he can to keep your son on the playing field."

Nope. Not the right answer. Eva signaled for a close-up. "You'll notice Dr. O'Donnell said there is much discussion over this topic. I, for one, would not put my child's life at risk over a school sport.

"But I completely understand your concern. It is very difficult to walk the line between keeping our children safe and letting them live a fulfilling life and developing the skills they need to become well-rounded adults. It is often a choice we have to make as parents."

Right there in front of her, ducked down below the camera lens, her producer was pointing to his watch and making a dramatic *cut* sign. Eva snuck a glance at the studio clock.

How had that happened? She had never run this long before.

"And that's a question each parent must answer for their children. Remember, moms, you can't take care of your children if you don't take care of yourselves first. So if you think you are having a heart attack, go to the emergency room."

She went into her sign-off. "Thanks for watching *Ask the Doc*. If you have questions, we have your answers. See you tomorrow."

She thought she'd done rather well at turning back to their topic of the day. Why, then, was her producer grimacing?

A closer look at the clock explained it—a minute over. The little red lights on the cameras went dark as Eva wondered which commercial they had cut. There would be an angry sponsor to answer to. They would have to offer them an extra slot to make up for it even though the show needed all the sponsors they could get. If they received any more production budget cuts, they'd have to start shooting the show with their camera phones.

Turning to Mark O'Donnell, Eva braced herself for saying the polite thing, even though he'd caused her show to be more topsy-turvy than a cheerleader doing backflips.

Trying to ignore the sexy way his shoulders filled out his lab coat, she said, "Thank you for—"

"You weren't serious, were you?"

What did he mean? "I'm sure I was. I always am."

Her husband had always encouraged her to lighten up, but it wasn't in her nature.

Her husband.

Finally, she could think about him without that tearing pain to her heart. If she could only find absolution for herself in her soul.

"What, in particular, were you referring to, Dr. O'Donnell?"

Maybe she'd had enough of his grandstanding in front of her audience, or maybe she was lashing out at him because of the hurt she still carried for her husband, but either way she lost her temper.

Gesturing off stage, she said, "Maybe you're talking about the way you came in an hour late and didn't have time for a pre-show briefing. Or the way you began to ad lib your presentation instead of following the bullet points. That could have ended up disastrously if either of our imaginations had failed us. Or how about that remark about me not being a real doctor?"

She took a breath, feeling her heart pound in her ears as well as in her chest.

"Or maybe you thought I wasn't serious when you decided to perform an examination on an audience member, while we all sat around and waited for you to listen to her heart beat. I'm sure our television audience enjoyed that stimulating bit of action. Or how about telling that father to go ahead and let his son do whatever he wanted despite the boy's doctor's advice. How dare you?"

Mark quirked his lips at her. "How dare I?"

"How dare you?" She was so angry she could feel the heat

radiate off her body. "How dare you undermine another doctor?"

"Somehow, I'm sure the boy's doctor won't mind."

"And you know that how?"

This time the man had the audacity to give her a full-on smile. "Because I'm him."

"What?"

"I'm the boy's doctor." Mark shrugged his massive shoulders. "I asked my friend to show up, you know, for moral support. He said if he saw the show faltering he'd ask a question and he did. Now I owe him a beer."

Eva stared, for once in her life without words. Her rage had burnt them all to cinders.

"It sounds like I owe you a beer, too, Eva. I didn't realize I was being such a screw-up."

"You are the last person I would consider sharing a beer with."

"Ouch." He gave her a laughing wince. "I guess that means, no, thanks."

"No, it doesn't mean, no, thanks. It means not in your lifetime, buddy."

"Alrighty, then." He looked at his watch. "Gotta run. It's been— I had thought this was fun, but it seems I was mistaken."

Was he expecting her to reassure him? She glared, daring him to blink first.

He didn't. Again there was that quirky twist of his lips, although this time they were tight instead of laughing. "It's been an experience."

As he turned to leave he stopped and raised an eyebrow, oh, so condescendingly. "You do pretty well for a TV doc."

CHAPTER TWO

"You've got to be kidding me." Eva paced round the conference table, earrings swinging as her agent cringed and her producer looked anywhere but in her eyes.

Stan, the show's executive producer, glared at her, too used to working with drama queens to be bothered by her display of temper, which made Eva even angrier. "A three-week series on high-school athletics to get the ratings up and get our audience used to field experience, then, if the ratings are high enough, you get your drug-abuse series. You've been asking for this and now you're complaining?"

"I didn't ask to work with someone I'm so obviously not compatible with, though."

"That's not what our audience surveys are saying. They loved Dr. O'Donnell and they loved the two of you together."

"Together." Eva stopped pacing to stare into Stan's eyes, gaining the slightest satisfaction that in her heels she towered over him. "I've worked hard for you. I've proved myself time and time again. O'Donnell waltzes onto the set, flashes a sexy grin and you beg him to take on a field assignment when I've been trying to negotiate one for the last two contracts?"

Phil, her daily producer and usually her ally, gathered up his courage to try to soothe her. "With sponsors pulling out, none of us have a lot of room for negotiation. We have to do something big to make up for cutting back our on-air schedule from five days to three."

"What? They're cutting our schedule?"

Phil seemed to shrink in on himself. "You didn't know?"

Both the producer and the executive producer stared at her agent as if her lack of easy agreement was all his fault.

She couldn't throw her kind-hearted agent under the bus.

"Henry's not to blame. I had to cancel our meeting yesterday." Her grandmother had been having a bad day, confused and agitated with all her caregivers. The sweet little lady who had raised her would never have raised her voice if she had been in her right mind. Dementia was a terrible disease.

And an expensive one to try to manage, too.

She needed this job. She had to remember that.

The money she could make by going back into clinical practice would easily take care of all her grandmother's needs with plenty left over. But she couldn't. She just couldn't. Not even for her *abuelita*.

"Talk to her," Stan demanded.

Henry sent them all a firm, noncommittal look. "Give us a moment."

Once the room was cleared, Eva leaned back in her chair, a feeling of unease building in the back of her neck. "What else haven't you told me?"

Mark O'Donnell watched his nephew run drills on the same high school field he'd once run them on. The coaches were new, but the discipline was the same.

Without sports and dedicated coaches to instill boundaries, Mark didn't know where he might have ended up.

Hopefully, he would provide a better father figure for Aaron than his absent dad had been.

"So she agreed?" Mark had been certain Eva Veracruz

would turn down the assignment faster than she could say manicure.

He still wasn't sure why he'd agreed himself. Maybe it had something to do with feeling more alive while on set than he had in a very long time.

Maybe that energy had more to do with Eva than it did with the television cameras. It was a question he didn't have to answer since the show and Eva went together.

And if she nixed the idea, he wouldn't have to worry about the why of it all, then, either, would he?

"She agreed," his newfound talent agent assured him. "She'll tape the shows live on Mondays and Wednesdays. You two will share a set on Fridays. And the rest of the time, for the next three weeks, she'll shadow you when you're doing your volunteer work at the high school, learning how you and the school system works with parents to keep our young athletes healthy both on and off the field. The executive producer wants to start filming on Tuesday."

Mark thought of how those boys on the field would react to having Eva in their locker room. Wasn't going to happen under his watch.

Second thoughts swamped him. He could hardly believe he was agreeing to do this. But he needed to break out of the rut he could see himself falling into and here was a sure-fire way to do that.

"I still find it hard to believe she graduated medical school, even though I looked up her bio on the station's web page." The bio's headline had read, *"Single, Sexy and Smart."* It had gone on to explain that Dr. Eva Veracruz was a New Orleans native with a degree in medicine from the state university. She'd been on the show for two years, having taken over from Dr. Todd Marsiglia.

Mark remembered Dr. Marsiglia's show. It had been dry, a filler for the thirty minutes before the noontime news. He'd often turned it on for the monotony to key down after the night shift.

"Did she even spend time practicing medicine before turning to television?"

Henry, who was also Eva's agent, shrugged. "I can't discuss that with you. Confidentiality. And I'd advise that you don't ask her about it either. Eva has some issues there."

"I'll just bet she does. She strikes me as the kind of woman that has issues about everything from her toenail polish to her hair color."

Henry gave him an unyielding frown, so unexpected from a man who made his living from negotiation and compromise. "There's more to Eva than most men bother to see."

"I've seen beneath the surface of women like her. I was married to a high-maintenance woman like Eva for longer than I care to admit." Mark realized he'd given his standard knee-jerk response. His statement wasn't the only thing jerky.

Apparently, not only had his ex destroyed his self-esteem, she'd turned him into a judgmental jerk, too.

Before Mark could retract his glib response, Henry gave one of his characteristic shrugs and turned the conversation. "You asked about the confidentiality of the students. Staff will need signed release waivers from anyone they film. For anyone under age, they'll need the waivers signed by either a parent or a legal guardian or we can't use the film. You can use that as a way to keep your interactions confidential if you need to."

"I understand. Thanks for checking on that for me."

"I consider it part of my job. Despite any preconceived ideas you have about us, agents really do take care of more than the paperwork."

"I'll remember that." Mark raised his hand in promise. "From now on, no preconceived ideas about agents or about doctors turned talk-show hosts."

Henry gave him a nod. "That would be a good thing to remember."

A good thing would be to wear sensible shoes on an athletic field. But Mark had stuck his own foot in his mouth enough already, so he refrained from saying it out loud as he watched Eva approach him.

To keep her heels from sinking into the grass, she had to take mincing steps on tiptoe, making her hips sway even more than he'd noticed earlier.

He'd always been a sucker for curvy women. His ex had cured him of a lot of his downfalls, but apparently not this one.

Mark had to exert great willpower to keep from gawking as Eva walked towards them.

Instead, he turned back toward the practice field where his nephew was now doing push-ups as punishment for some transgression, likely mouthing off. Mark worried about the boy. Aaron was too much like him at that age. The kid was going to get into real trouble if he didn't change his ways.

But no amount of advice was going to keep Aaron safe from himself. Again, experience talking.

Mark gave the assistant coach a nod and a knowing look, even though the man wouldn't see it with his attention focused on Aaron. If not for the dedication of men like him, *he* wouldn't be who he was. He didn't know how he would have turned out without such dedicated role models, he only knew he would have become someone a lot, lot worse.

Aaron had a good heart. But he also had a hot head. Between his mouthiness and his temper, he was too much of a handful for Mark's sister to handle along with her new husband.

In the three months since Aaron had moved in with him, Mark's grocery bill had quadrupled, his electricity bill had doubled and his social life had become non-existent.

Which explained why the Hispanic hottie in front of him captured more of his interest than he wanted to give her.

Time for a date night. What did he do with that cute little history teacher's number?

Eva pointed her clipboard at him. "I'm only doing this for the numbers."

"What numbers?"

"Ratings." She looked out at the field then back at him. "Let's get this right out in the open. It wasn't my idea to partner with you, but I'm a professional and intend to make the best of it. I'm hoping you'll extend me the same *professional* courtesy."

Mark knew what she was referring to. "Professional courtesy like acknowledging your medical degree?"

"That's a start."

"I looked you up. You're legitimate."

"I looked you up, too." She gave him a hard stare up and down. "You do a lot of volunteer work for the local high schools, this school in particular. You're well respected among the educators and the coaches in the area. I'm impressed with your work."

He hadn't been expecting a compliment. "Thanks."

"But you need to understand from the beginning that I'm the lead on this project. Got it?"

"Got it." Mark gritted his teeth. It went against his nature to follow anyone's lead. But his years in sports had taught him how to be a team player even if he couldn't always be team captain.

Apparently, his tone didn't convince her, because Eva put her hands on her hips, straining the fabric across her breasts as she drove her point home. "Those tricks you learned for getting through those five-minute press-release interviews you did when you were in high school won't always save you when you have to fill a thirty-minute segment."

She was a lot of woman. Swimsuit model came to mind—not the über-skinny kind selling women's fashions but the kind that made it into men's sports magazines, the kind that were substantial enough for a real man to put his hands on.

Women had always complimented his large hands.

He concentrated on her mouth instead. But those full red lips were as much of a distraction as the two buttons that threatened to pop.

Eyes, Mark. Look in her eyes and no lower.

"Are you listening to me, O'Donnell? This is a topic I'm very passionate about."

Those flashing black eyes echoed her words. Yes, she was a passionate woman.

"Don't worry, Dr. Veracruz. I'm a big fan of passion."

Her brow furrowed, warning him she was readying herself for another impassioned lecture. As much as he would enjoy watching her deliver it, he also respected what she'd said.

"Give me a chance to try again with a better reply." He was usually quicker thinking on his feet than this. He held up a hand, buying time as he gathered his thoughts.

"I have to admit, if you hadn't stepped in and helped when I was explaining the heart-attack symptoms, I would have been sunk." Mark always gave credit where credit was due. "To do this series the way it needs to be done, I'm going to need your experience."

Eva was a sucker for a man who admitted he needed her. But Mark O'Donnell would be her exception. He was one of those kinds of men all smart women avoided, the kind of man who would scramble your brain and break your heart.

And she hadn't yet got her mind straightened out from the last man she'd given her heart to.

Automatically her fingers felt for the missing wedding band that held a special place in her jewelry box. Almost two years.

The pain had finally become a dull thud instead of a sharp ache.

"Bad break-up?" Mark noticed her hands. He seemed to notice everything.

"You could say that."

But she wasn't about to trip down memory lane with this man in front of her.

"I really don't want to talk about it."

Maybe she would talk about it one day, but not today and not to this man.

Her camera crew awaited her signal as they sat in their steaming van on the coaches' parking lot. Mid-September with both the temperature and humidity in the high nineties didn't make waiting a pleasure.

She gave them a big wave and they tumbled out, dragging equipment with them.

Mark glared at them. "What's this?"

"We're here to get filler video, get the feel of the environment, maybe do an impromptu interview or two, that kind of thing."

"I just agreed to do this show with you. How have you come already prepared?"

"It was happening with or without you."

"So should I think of myself as expendable or as a bonus?"

"Whatever floats your boat, baby." There went the sarcasm again.

He arched his eyebrow at her. "Baby?"

The second she'd called him "baby", she'd known she shouldn't have. But she knew how to handle men like this one. She looked him straight in the eye, challenging him. "You're not going to file a sexual harassment complaint against me, are you?"

"Not if you promise to kiss me next time you call me

'baby'. After all, if you're going to sweet-talk me, I think I should get the whole benefit of it."

"Fine." She shouldn't have said that. But it had been a while since she'd done anything she shouldn't. And the man intrigued her. Few men did.

She widened her eyes and leaned forward, knowing he would respond to her body language. "Anything to get out of all the paperwork your complaint would cause me."

Without waiting for his retort, she turned towards her crew, who were setting up with a good view of the practice field in the background.

A bead of sweat rolled down her cleavage, tickling her sensitive skin. With a clear conscience she could blame it entirely on the heat. She had always been a cool one with men and this man would be no exception.

But they'd need make-up to cover the effects of the temperature on both of them. Sweat beaded on his brow. She could feel similar beads on her upper lip. How would Dr. Mark O'Donnell feel about heavy-duty face powder?

She saw the crew's make-up artist walking towards him, and saw Mark wave the woman away. This could get interesting.

Instead, Mark walked toward the canopy set up at the end of the practice field just as one of the coaches blew his whistle.

The boys scurried to the canopy, jostling each other as they queued up.

As they received sports drinks or water, Mark would occasionally pat one on the shoulder and point toward a bench in the shade. Near the end of the line, one of the larger boys tried to protest. Even from this distance Eva could see Mark's stance stiffen as he stared the boy down.

After a tense two seconds it was over. The boy stomped past the bench to the field house, teenage anger apparent in every line of his body.

The incident seemed to take the energy from the team as adult shoulders squared and teenage shoulders drooped all around. Eva could almost smell the testosterone in the air.

Unlike the football team, her video team was jazzed up and raring to go.

"Ready, Eva?" her cameraman asked. He was a veteran at field assignments and excited to be out of the studio.

She took the huge directional microphone from a gaffer and planted her feet.

"Ready."

Her producer counted her down, "On three, two, one…"

Eva put on her television smile and resisted looking around for Mark. It seemed she would be working without a partner today.

"As promised, we're at a local high school, checking out their sports program. With temperatures often over one hundred degrees, many of you are asking why the football team would hold practice today. Others are remembering their own high-school football days and beginning of the school year practices. And we're all asking today on *Ask the Doc*, 'Is it safe for our teens to physically exert themselves in this heat?'"

Before Eva could launch into her opinion, her cameraman pulled from her and changed his focus.

Eva turned to see where his lens now pointed. Mark was squatting down, looking into the faces of the boys on the bench, who had taken off their shoulder pads.

The rest of the boys, also sans shoulder pads, did crunches on the field as their coaches walked among them.

One of the coaches barked an order and they all rolled over for push-ups.

The producer pointed at her and mouthed, low enough her microphone wouldn't pick it up, "Ready."

She gave a silent nod and put on her media face once again.

"As you can see behind me, the boys on this team are

monitored for dehydration and overheating. There are many heat-related conditions that can occur. Among the most dangerous is heatstroke, which can result in brain damage and even death."

"That's a cut."

She nodded, satisfied. She'd left herself a good transition. Once in the studio and on set, she could go into the various signs and symptoms of heat cramp and heat exhaustion and the emergency medical actions to take. The information would be accompanied by several of the brightly colored bullet-point charts and visual presentations her audiences grasped so well.

Possessiveness swamped her. She'd worked hard to develop the show into an educational yet entertaining program. And now she had to share with a man who couldn't even be counted on to stand still long enough for a three-minute field interview.

Mark trotted back towards Eva, frowning at the crew, who were packing up. He glanced at his bare wrist for the watch he never wore. Time in the E.R. went at its own pace and no amount of ticking second hands could speed it up or slow it down.

Apparently, television didn't work like the real world.

"I missed it?"

She looked down her nose at him as only a tall woman could. "You missed it."

"I was only gone a few minutes."

"We only needed a few minutes of footage. Now the crew has to go back to the studio and do edits, sound adjustments, tie-ins to tomorrow's show, the whole bit." She gave him a patronizing smile. "You can't be expected to know any of this with your lack of experience."

She was right. But it still stung.

That drive to be the one in the know, to be top of his class, to handle whatever was thrown at him was the inner force that made him focus when his world was in total chaos around him. He knew how to win.

But he also knew how to be gracious. Experience had taught him that.

"I'm hoping to learn a lot from you."

She tilted her head sideways, studying him. "I can't figure you out."

"Nothing to figure out." He held his arms out wide. "What you see is what you get."

"That's it? Surface deep?" She gave him a cheeky grin. "Shallow?"

"Woman, you can twist words better than any fancy Southern lawyer I've ever known."

"I just call 'em like I see 'em."

"There are some men who like their women sharp-witted and sharp-tongued."

"But you're not one of them?"

"I didn't say that." He fought hard to keep the grin off his face. That was exactly how he liked his women.

But his ex *was* a fancy Southern lawyer. And Mark *did* learn from experience, especially bad experiences.

"So what are you saying?"

"Just that I plan to get as much as I can out of this television gig. Never can tell when the experience will come in handy."

A very large teen came loping up the hill. Eva was almost certain he was the boy who'd been sent off the field.

"Hey, Uncle Mark. All-you-can-eat pizza tonight, right? Ready to go?"

Mark gave him a thumbs-up. "I'm ready. I just hope the pizza parlor is ready for us."

Eva squinted at the boy. He was almost as tall and just as wide as Mark. The family resemblance was strong.

As Aaron got closer to her, she saw a glassy glint in his eye that she'd seen before, a glint that promised unpredictability and that made her instinctively brace herself for whatever action the boy might take. "Aaron, say hello to Dr. Veracruz."

"Hi." The boy held out a huge, sweaty palm to shake her hand.

Eva fought back her natural instinct to withdraw, to protect herself.

Face your fears, Eva. That's what her husband would say to her. But, then, she'd never been frightened when Chuck had been around. Experience had taught her differently.

She grasped his hand firmly in her own. "Nice to meet you."

Aaron squeezed the slightest bit too tight, like a boy who wasn't used to his own strength. Common enough at his age, right?

Eva tried to quell her worries. Maybe she was reading her own fear into her snap judgment.

And that's why she'd pulled herself out of the field of drug and substance abuse care. Her judgment, so critical for making evaluations, was too clouded by personal emotion to be trusted.

"So, Doc, you want to eat pizza with Uncle Mark and me?"

Mark clapped his nephew on the shoulder. "No one could accuse my nephew of being shy."

"No, he's certainly not shy."

Mark added his own invitation. "So how about it? It's just pizza."

She was usually so good with snap decisions—but that had been before. She'd promised her sister-in-law she'd embrace life in all its aspects, including enjoying the company of nice, respectful men. They all agreed her husband would never have wanted her to wallow in her widowhood.

And the deep, gut-wrenching sadness had faded, leaving lonely nostalgia behind.

"Afraid you'll fall for my charm and wit?"

"No." *Maybe.* Eva wasn't sure what she was afraid of. Her sister-in-law would say Eva was afraid of risking her heart again. But it was only pizza.

"No? That's it? Nothing to soften the blow?"

"Somehow I think your ego is healthy enough to survive."

Aaron rubbed his hand across his brow. "I don't know about that, Doc. His divorce hit him pretty hard."

Mark glared at his nephew as he brushed him on the back of the head. "No one could accuse my nephew of being discreet either."

Aaron shrugged, looking confused. "Just trying to help."

"Well, don't." He dug in his pocket and handed his nephew the car keys. "I'm parked in visitor parking. Pull the truck around to the stadium parking lot—and don't pull out onto the street. Don't race the engine. Don't—"

"Don't breathe wrong. I got it." With a tight jaw Aaron snagged the keys then took off at an irritated run.

What turned the tide on her decision? Was it the glimpse of vulnerability and sadness she'd seen in Mark's eyes? Or was it the way his biceps flexed. Either way, she said, "Fine. I'll come."

Now Mark narrowed his gaze at her. "I don't need a pity date."

"That's good since I don't do pity dates. I only do pepperoni, extra onions."

"Extra onions? You don't do goodnight kisses either, then, do you?"

"Never on a first date to a pizza parlor."

"Is it the venue? You need a more upscale wine-and-dinery?"

"Nope. It's the first date thing. Why waste a good kiss if I'm not sure about a second date yet?"

"Right. Because kisses are in limited supply?"

She cocked an eyebrow at him. "Mine are rare, which makes them extremely valuable."

"Then I'll treasure them properly, should I ever decide to accept one."

"*Should* you decide?" She gave him her best smoldering look along with a very deliberate lip lick. "I could make you beg."

"I'd like to see you try." His answer was flippant but the widening of his pupils told another story. Eva would bet anything his pulse was racing.

At least she wasn't lusting alone. She found herself leaning forward, as if she were being sucked toward him.

The moment was so on the verge she forgot she was standing on a high-school athletic field until a half-dozen cheerleaders walked past, giggling and posturing for the boys, who were obviously waiting for them.

Aaron honked the horn, waving to the girls. One broke free from the gaggle to wander over to where he hung out of the truck window.

"Yours?" she called to him as she pointed to the truck.

"My uncle lets me drive it whenever I want to."

The girl propped one hand on her hip, emphasizing the shortness of her cheerleading skirt. "Nice. Give me a ride?"

Even from a distance Eva could interpret the scowl Aaron sent Mark. "I didn't bring my license today."

She twirled her finger into her hair. "Bring it tomorrow and I'll let you drive me home."

The girl gave a saucy toss of her hair then turned to walk back toward her friends. Three steps away, she stopped and looked over her shoulder to make sure Aaron was watching her.

He was.

Sotto voce, Mark said, for Eva's ears only, "He doesn't have his license. I'm not sure how I can help him save face on this one."

"Some things a man has to learn how to do for himself." It's what her husband had said whenever she'd wanted to save her brother from himself.

Mark gave her an irritated, challenging look before taking a step away from her. "What would you know about that?"

Now two men needed their egos stroked.

All she'd agreed to was pizza.

"Tell you what, Mark. I'll drive my own car and meet you there."

As she walked away, Eva resisted the pull to look over her shoulder to see if Mark was watching her walk away.

But she did indulge in a come-hither hair-twirl.

CHAPTER THREE

EVA WALKED BACK to her car, amazed at herself. What had just happened to her? She hadn't flirted like that since—since high school?

But it had felt so good.

Chuck. Now the feelings of disloyalty hit her.

Not that Chuck wouldn't want her to move on with her life.

Chuck had never indulged in flirting. One of the hazards of dating and then marrying an older man, she'd always thought.

Older man—ha!

Chuck had been younger than Mark when they'd started dating all those years ago. At her ripe old age of eighteen she'd thought him much older at eight years her senior.

He had given her the security she'd craved, the safety she'd needed, and the love she'd worked so hard to return in equal measure. Even if that had meant suppressing her wild side to fit into Chuck's world.

He'd never asked her to change. But she had, thinking she owed it to him to become a part of his straight-up world.

But now Chuck was gone and all she was left with was her own world, a world she could define any way she wanted to, if she only had the courage.

Eva squared her shoulders.

"Bring it on," she said to the universe at large.

You're the only one who can hold you back, she heard, as if Chuck were sitting next to her.

She smiled, hearing the wisdom in the words Chuck would have said to her.

She thought about Mark. Thought about the flirting. Thought about the way she'd felt so alive as she'd teased and sparred. Thought about what could happen next.

And tried to bury all her angst, all her worry and fear of being hurt again. Tried to be brave, as she said aloud, "Let's do this."

A strong sense of approval passed through her, leaving her feeling warm inside.

While the logical part of Mark regretted asking Eva to join him, his baser libido couldn't help watching her backside swing as she made her way to her car.

It was a little convertible. Black. Impractical with the frequent storms and the excessive heat of New Orleans, but it fit her.

Was she as impractical as her car? At first glance, a man might think so. But the intelligence behind those heavily mascaraed eyelashes made him cautious about underestimating her.

With the hard lessons his ex-wife had given him about the dangers of a beautiful woman with brains, anyone would think he'd turn and walk—no, run—in the opposite direction. Apparently, he was a slow learner.

Still, who was she to offer parenting advice? She had no children. None listed in her bio, anyway.

But she did have gorgeous child-bearing hips.

He walked up to the driver's side of his truck, opened the door and motioned Aaron out.

"Let me drive, Uncle Mark. Just up to the pizza place."

Here came the hard part of parenting. The tough-love part. "No way. You blew that privilege out of the water."

"It wasn't my fault."

That was the statement Aaron kept repeating over and over. Not his fault. And that was the attitude that kept Mark worried about his nephew. Being too immature to own his transgressions meant the boy was too immature to learn from his mistakes.

Mark didn't let the remark go unchecked. He'd tried that before and Aaron had taken the silent approach to mean his uncle had believed him.

"That's right, Aaron. Those other boys tackled you and poured beer down your throat and there was nothing you could do about it. And then they forced you to get into that car and drive twenty miles over the speed limit with police cars behind you flashing their lights for over a half mile before one finally pulled in front of you and made you pull over."

Mark gave Aaron his best sarcastic cynicism, one of the few tones of voice Aaron seemed to listen to. "So what part of that wasn't your fault?"

Instead of hanging his head in shame, as he had first done when the whole incident had happened, Aaron glared at his uncle. The fierce anger in his eyes gave Mark real worry.

What was happening to that chubby-cheeked little boy his sister had given birth to seventeen years ago?

Silently, Aaron turned to stare out the window, his jaw jutting, his forehead creased, fury in every line of his body.

Mark knew all about being a teenager with a new stepfather in the house. The clashing of two male egos made for a lot of angst and anger.

But Mark had taken all his pent-up energy to the football field and had left it there, thanks to a few great coaches who had taught their players as many life lessons as sports plays.

Still, he'd said too many things he still regretted and it was now too late to apologize to his mother and his stepfather, the man who had done his best to make her happy.

That's why he'd volunteered to take Aaron into his home. To try to make amends for his own youth.

Maybe he was looking back through self-forgiving lenses, but he didn't remember being as cruel and as crude as Aaron had been to his mother. The boy showed no respect. And Mark's meek, mild sister didn't know how to command it.

What would Eva do? She was a talk-show host. She'd probably try to talk reason to the boy.

Mark had talked until his throat ached. If the right words existed to get through to Aaron, Mark certainly didn't know them.

Somehow he didn't think Eva would put up with the poor behavior his sister accepted. There was something in the set of her jaw and the directness of her gaze.

As they pulled into the parking lot, Aaron's scowl morphed into one of anticipation. The boy couldn't get enough food.

Even though the pizza buffet offered all-you-can-eat servings, Mark felt like he should pay for two meals for Aaron.

As a physician, Mark had seen a lot of adolescent growth spurts and Aaron's ranked at the top of the charts.

While Aaron was growing taller, he was growing wider at a faster rate. Football and independent workouts in the weight room were turning all his new-found weight into muscle. When his size caught up to his breadth, the boy would be an imposing young man. He had to get that raging temper of his under control before then.

But Aaron's mercurial mood had turned into all smiles when he piled out of the truck and headed toward the group of cheerleaders who were waiting outside the door of the pizza place for the boys to show up.

He felt his own mood turn into anticipation once he spotted Eva opening her car door. Her skirt rode up to show off her long, athletic legs as she climbed from the low-slung car.

He hurried over to give her a hand, giving him a chance to get an up-close look at the silky skin her skirt exposed.

When he ran his hands up and down those thighs, he knew they would feel as smooth and firm as they looked. And her hands on him would feel—

He'd thought he'd outgrown his teenage impulsiveness, but around Eva his libido was still at its pubescent peak.

She took his outstretched palm, sending pulses straight to his primal brain center and setting off a chain reaction.

He pulled her up a little too hard, a little too strong, knocking her off balance on those teetering heels.

When she put her other hand on his chest to steady herself she set his heart beating so strongly she couldn't help but feel it even through his shirt.

Her nails were trim and unpolished. Medical-practice standards. He'd expected a fancy manicure like—

But Eva wasn't his ex, who had indulged in having her nails done at least once a week.

He hadn't spent this much time thinking about his ex since the divorce had been finalized. Why now?

And why was he comparing Eva to her?

Because he was trying to find a reason to steer clear of Eva. Judging Eva against another woman wasn't fair to her. He wouldn't want to be compared to another man. He owed it to her to find out who she really was.

"Sorry." Eva jerked her hand back from Mark's chest.

She almost fell backwards as she tried to right herself.

He put his arm around her, pulling her close to steady her.

What was it about him that kept her so off balance?

He was strong enough, big enough to keep them both on

their feet, which was saying a lot. She was not some delicate little daisy of a woman. Few men could handle her so easily.

She had felt this secure in Chuck's arms, too.

"Sorry," she repeated as she pushed away, this time more cautiously even though she wanted to quickly put distance between herself and that intense, pulsing energy Mark exuded before she lost more than her balance.

Common sense was hard to come by when in the arms of such a testosterone-laden man.

He was full of life, she could feel it in him.

She'd always liked the type of man who lived life to the fullest. Until that kind of living had got her husband killed.

While she had promised herself that she would honor Chuck's memory by going on with life, she hadn't promised to fall for the same kind of guy.

Only pizza. Not a date. If she kept repeating that over and over, she should be fine.

Cars, most with school stickers in their windows, were parked haphazardly in the parking lot. Threading through them took a bit of skill.

Most of the cars were relatively new, testimony to the wealth of the high school's neighborhood. In her old high school neighborhood, it had usually been the drug dealers who'd had the nice cars. What would Mark think of her if he knew where she'd come from?

What did it matter?

She was so busy trying to be unaffected by the man at her side she almost walked into a trailer hitch extending from an oversized truck. A quick dodge saved her from a bruised shin and also earned her Mark's hand on her elbow, guiding her.

She should shrug it off.

Mark was a co-worker, a temporary one at that. She would get to know him because that would make working with him smoother and that would be that.

And they could use more than a little smoothing out in the work department.

She'd already had a phone call from her producer. He wasn't pleased Mark hadn't been in the segment. As the experienced host, it was her job to make sure they shared the limelight in the taped shots and on their Friday live show.

She was expected to rectify that in their next taping the following afternoon.

But first she had to get through this dinner she should have turned down.

Except her apartment was so quiet. So empty. So lifeless.

If she could have, she would have stopped by the hospital to rock the babies in Neonatal. Those little ones going through withdrawal from their addicted mothers could always use a calming touch.

But her touch was no longer calm, not when she smelled the hospital's antiseptic or heard the intercom system calling codes.

It had been two years since she'd passed through the sliding glass doors of the place where she'd found such satisfaction in fulfilling her life's purpose. Two years. Way past time to move on.

Maybe she would try it this weekend. Of course, she'd told herself that same thing last weekend and the weekend before that, too.

"What? Is something wrong?" Mark asked, bringing her back to herself.

"I'm fine. Why would you ask?" she challenged him, but she knew his answer. She'd gone tense. Her pulse had started to race. Her breathing had quickened.

It wouldn't have taken an E.R. doctor to figure out something was wrong.

"You stopped walking." He stated the obvious.

"I've got a rock in my shoe." She bent to adjust her shoe,

all too aware of his hand holding her steady while she shook out the non-existent rock.

With astonishment, Eva recognized the firmness of his hand steadied her mentally as well as physically. She had been numb for so long.

Mark opened the door for her and she realized how long it had been since she'd enjoyed the niceties of a man-woman relationship, too.

Not that this was one. But she could still appreciate the etiquette, couldn't she?

Mark picked out a table for them in a nook far away from the cluster of tables the teens had pushed together.

"Seen but not heard," he said. "I want to make sure he knows I'm keeping an eye on him."

Only a sparse handful of adults were present and they certainly weren't hovering like Mark was.

While she'd never had money for pizza at Aaron's age, she remembered gathering together with her friends without such strict supervision. Was that why Aaron was so angry? His uncle held too tight a rein on him?

Not her business. She had enough family of her own to worry about. She didn't need to add her co-worker's family to her list.

"Help yourself at the pizza bar," their server said as she took their drinks order.

Eva had expected Mark to order a beer. It's what Chuck had always done on pizza night. Instead, he ordered sweet tea, just like she did.

Eva stopped herself right there. She would not compare every man she met to Chuck. Her husband was gone and there would never be another one just like him.

As the servers brought out fresh pizzas, the teens swarmed the buffet bar, jostling each other as if they hadn't eaten in a week.

"Should we wait until they finish?" Eva looked toward the bar.

"If we do, we might never get to eat." Mark swiped her plate from in front of her along with his own. "Pepperoni and onion, right?"

"Yes. You remembered."

He gave her an open smile. "Wish me luck. I'm going in."

Eva watched with admiration as Mark politely and authoritatively broached the crowd to snag enough pizza for their supper.

"Madam." With a flourish, he set her plate in front of her. "If this isn't enough, I can go in for more."

Eva had always had a healthy appetite, more so than her petite friends, and it looked like Mark had judged her just right. "Two pieces. Perfect."

Mark also had two pieces of Sweep the Swamp pizza, along with a side order of bread sticks with extra marinara sauce for dipping. He obviously liked his pizza with everything on it, including shrimp and crawfish tails.

"I'll share these." He pushed the plate of breadsticks her way.

"I'm good with what I have. Thanks." Contentedness filled her as she realized she spoke the truth about more than pizza. Right now, at this moment, she was good with what she had.

"Wow." Mark widened his eyes at her.

"Wow, what?"

"That's one beautiful smile you keep hidden there, lady."

Yes, she was smiling. Eva felt the fullness of her cheeks and the lightness in her heart.

And a warmth, as if Chuck were there, approving of her, of this, of Mark.

She hid behind a slice of pizza, letting the feeling sink in. "Thank you."

"My pleasure." Mark dipped a breadstick and gestured to the pizza bar. "The locusts have swarmed."

The bar held nothing but empty platters and a single upside-down piece of pizza.

The volume from the teens' tables was muted as they dug into their food.

Eva watched as a cheerleader picked a slice of pepperoni from her pizza, studied it, then nibbled half of it before putting it back on her plate.

Next to her, Aaron scoffed down his own overflowing plate. From the looks of things, he wasn't picky about the kind of pizza he preferred as long as it was edible.

Mark saw what caught her attention. "I used to eat like that. But those days ended when my football days did."

"Did you play college ball, too?"

"I wanted to, but I couldn't keep my grades up and play football. Too many hours of practice. Too many missed classes when travelling to the games. The coaches said I could have gone pro. Maybe. Maybe not. Now I'll never know." Uncertainty shadowed his eyes. "It was a hard choice."

"What made you choose medicine?"

"All the wrong reasons."

"Such as…?"

"My dad's a doctor. I thought if I followed in his footsteps, maybe he'd approve. Maybe he'd be proud." Mark put down the breadstick he'd not taken a bite from. "What are you? Some kind of hypnotist? I'm telling you things I never even told my ex-wife. And we've just met."

"Maybe it was just the right time to say it out loud." Eva searched for the right thing to say that respected his revelations but didn't encourage more of them.

While she admired his honesty, she felt uncomfortable with it. She didn't want to be this man's confessor. She couldn't handle her own past pain much less anyone else's.

At least, that's what she'd been telling herself all these months.

But she had been born to listen, to draw out hidden hurts, to help heal them. It was a part of her, the reason she'd done well as a substance abuse specialist. Knowing that Mark found that in her gave her hope that she hadn't lost that major part of herself.

But she had successfully broken the mood. She could see that in Mark's body language as he leaned back in his chair and looked past her, glancing around the room instead of meeting her eyes.

There was that lopsided, subtle smile again.

His crooked half was one part plastic politeness, and the other part regret that he had revealed such a tender part of himself to her.

"In the end, it was a good decision. I don't think I could have kept up the drive to play professionally through all the injuries those guys sustain. I like waking up in the mornings knowing my knees will bend and my back will straighten."

She shouldn't ask. She shouldn't turn the conversation deeper while he was trying to lighten the mood, but she asked anyway. "And medicine? Was that a good decision?"

Mark grinned, a real one this time as his eyes sparkled. "I love the E.R. The challenges, the pace, pulling off the occasional miracle. Growing up, I never related to my dad. But once I started practicing medicine, I finally understood what drove him. That satisfaction of making people better. I can't imagine doing anything else."

Eva had felt like that once. Glorying in that satisfaction of making people better. But now she was afraid she'd never feel like that again.

He held up a piece of pizza. "My turn to eat. Your turn to talk. So what about you? Why did you choose your profession over sports?"

"You ask that sarcastically, don't you?"

He cocked an eyebrow at her. "I just can't imagine you sweating."

"Then you need to expand your imagination." She gave a moment's pause along with a flirty grin before she defended her athletic prowess. "I was pretty good at basketball."

"How good?" he challenged. Everything about this man seemed to be a challenge.

"Sports scholarship material." But she'd turned it down. Chuck had insisted on carrying the financial burden, supplementing her academic scholarships by working overtime as often as he'd been able to get the hours and signing on for student loans even though he'd known it would put them in debt for years.

Investing in their future, he used to say.

"So you played basketball through college?"

"Nope. As good as I was at basketball, I was better at books. Academic scholarship." She fluffed her hair, knowing it would distract him. "Besides, to practice medicine, I don't have to sweat the way I do when I practice sports. And my hair is a mess when I sweat."

He leaned in and leered. "I wouldn't mind seeing you sweat."

"Yeah?"

"Yeah. We could have a friendly game of one on one."

A totally different kind of one on one popped into Eva's head, just as Mark had intended, she was sure.

"We're talking basketball, right?"

He looked mock surprised. "Of course. What else would I be talking about?"

She wasn't sure what made her say it, but she answered his challenge. "You're on, buddy. Any time. Anywhere."

"That's what I like to hear."

Eva started to rethink her rashness. Too much, too soon.

But she'd promised her sister-in-law, Susan. She'd promised to accept invitations. To stay out of her apartment as much as possible. To stop brooding by herself in the dark. She'd promised to try.

She hid her uncertainty behind a flirty wink. "You bring the ball and your A-game."

"I always do."

Eva found herself gazing into Mark's eyes, trying to figure out if they were more bronze than green as light flickered in their depths. Fascinating.

"Excuse me, aren't you Dr. Veracruz from the TV show?" an elderly woman interrupted. Eva hadn't even realized the woman was there. How much had she heard?

While Eva didn't often have fans interrupt her supper, it did occasionally happen. In front of Mark, it made her feel pretty proud.

"Yes, I am."

"I hate to bother you but my friend and I saw your show on heart attacks and she thinks she's having one."

Eva looked to where the woman pointed to see another elderly lady sweating profusely through her gray complexion.

Immediately, she was on her feet and rushing over to the table.

She felt Mark right behind her.

"Call 911," she directed the elderly woman. "Then bring us the phone."

Mark helped the woman out of the booth and onto the floor as Eva dug in her purse for an aspirin.

As Mark found the woman's pulse, Eva put the aspirin into the elderly lady's mouth.

"Chew it up, honey. That's the way," she murmured encouragingly.

She heard Mark talk to the emergency dispatcher, who was pushing the call through to the emergency personnel.

Eva could already hear the ambulance's siren getting closer as Mark updated them on the woman's vitals.

Within seconds, the emergency crew was there with their stretcher.

"Mira thought she was having indigestion. But I watch your show every day, Dr. Veracruz. And I remembered what you and this young fellow said."

"We're ready to roll," one of the paramedics said to the elderly friend. "You can ride with us, ma'am."

And just like that, it was over.

Mark gave her a deep, thorough look. "Your show just saved a life."

Great happiness bloomed inside her, happiness bordering on euphoria. "Yes, it did."

His eyes sparkled as they gazed into hers. They were so clear. So bright. So alive.

Then the sound of chairs being scraped back from the teens' tables broke through her fixation.

Mark blinked, releasing her from his stare.

"It's curfew for most of these kids." He looked down at his watch, giving her a sheepish glance from under his lashes. "I guess I lost track of time and you haven't finished your meal."

Eva's pizza had cooled and congealed, making it totally unappealing. "I've had plenty. In fact, I don't think I could take in another thing tonight."

The effects of her emotions filled her more than food ever could.

Mark nodded as if he understood the full meaning behind her words. "Me, too."

He stood and pulled her chair for her. "When will I see you again?"

His voice, coming from behind her, so low and deep, sent shivers through her. She swallowed twice and concentrated on his question.

"Tomorrow after the show the camera crew and I will tape a few more segments. What time will you be able to join us?"

"Since I've got the night shift, I'll go in to the hospital a couple of hours from now. After my shift, I'll run home and catch a little sleep before I join you in the late afternoon."

Eva hadn't even thought about how Mark would work his regular schedule around his filming schedule. "How will this work for Fridays when we tape mid-morning?"

"I'll leave straight from work for the studio."

He'd been late last Friday for his guest shot. Had the producers thought of all that could go wrong here?

Eva had to remind herself that Mark's scheduling wasn't her problem even though covering for him was her responsibility if he didn't make it on time.

Mark gave her a cocky grin. "Don't worry. It will all work out."

That's what Chuck used to say. But she was a worrier and a pre-planner. And it hadn't all worked out.

All the worrying in the world hadn't prepared her for the shooting that had taken his life.

"I could, couldn't I, Uncle Mark?" Aaron called to them from the front door of the pizza parlor, several yards away.

"You could what, Aaron?"

"I could pull an airplane like that guy on that reality show." The shadows cast by the fading sunset hid the boy's acne and called attention to his profile, only slightly similar to his uncle's.

The braggadocio was typical of a teenage boy. Her brother had thought he was invincible at that age, too.

Eva shouldn't count it as a symptom, shouldn't suspect— that's why she was on leave. PTSD affected her ability to make the kinds of diagnoses a substance abuse specialist needed to make.

Mark was a doctor. He would see the signs in his nephew if there were any to see, wouldn't he?

No, he wouldn't. Not if he was like most relatives. Steroid abuse was one of those problems that could too easily be mistaken for teenage angst.

"I'll walk you to your car." Mark put his hand on her elbow, making her feel secure in the falling twilight.

"You don't have to," she said from the habit of asserting her independence, *but she wanted him to.*

"I want to."

Deep inside, that felt good. "Okay."

Outside her car, she clicked the locks open and he opened the door for her.

Bracketed between her open car door and Mark, she turned and looked up to thank him for the lovely evening, as her grandmother would expect her to.

His lips were a mere fraction of an inch from hers. It would be so easy. One little word and she could remember what if felt like to be desired. To be wanted. To be touched. To feel the power of being a woman again.

"Thanks," she whispered, "baby." With the slightest of movements, she closed the gap.

Mark's lips met hers. Tender. Masculine. And, oh, so needed. That's what his kiss was.

Her mind went spinning off the earth as her body leaned into him without her consent. His arms came around her, pulling her even closer.

The scent of him filled her, every cell of her. His taste fed her, giving sustenance to the part of her that had starved for so long.

His moan mingled with hers, creating a harmony she had only felt with—

Abruptly, her body was under her control again. Guilt

swamped her as she realized the last man she'd kissed like that had been her husband.

She didn't even know Mark.

She put her hands between them, pushing him away.

He looked up, his eyes dazed. "What?"

"I don't know why I..." She looked past him, to the rising star behind his shoulder. "It's not a—"

"Date," he finished for her. "Only pizza."

"Only pizza," she echoed, still not thinking straight.

"For the record, I like the taste of onions. At least, I do when I taste them on you."

"I've got to go." She had no need to be anywhere. She just knew she didn't need to be here.

He gave her more space by checking the time on his phone. "Me, too. Got to get the kid home then on to work."

"Okay, then." She slid into her car seat and buckled her seat belt, then firmly put her hands on the steering wheel.

"Okay, then." He started to close her car door for her, but paused. "See you tomorrow."

"Tomorrow." Her powers of higher-level speech seemed to be totally banished to that place she'd lived in before his kiss. That place she needed to get back to right now.

"Mark?"

"Yes, Eva?"

"This won't affect our work, will it?"

Mark's face, even softened by dusk, went stone cold. "No. It won't affect our work."

Click. Her mind slid back into place with a harsh snap.

"Okay, then. See you tomorrow," she repeated to him, but in a purely professional, no-nonsense tone.

With a nod he closed the door between them, ending their date that wasn't a date with a finality that made her feel as if she'd just been startled awake from a lovely dream.

Would this dream fade from her memory like the ones where Chuck visited her just before she awoke in the morning?

It would have to. She needed to be focused, sharp, fully grounded in reality to do her job. And her job was all she had.

CHAPTER FOUR

Mark didn't have to tell Aaron to abandon the driver's seat and take the passenger seat instead. His scowl was fierce enough that even his rebellious nephew didn't argue.

Despite Aaron's preference for country music, Mark tuned the radio to screaming rock and cranked it up loud. The driving beat surrounded him, matching his mood exactly. But the heavy metal guitars and pounding drums couldn't beat the feeling of stupidity from his head.

He knew better! He knew better and had done it anyway. He had let himself be attracted to a woman just like the last one.

Saying he was holding her back in her career, Tiffany had left him with nothing but a broken heart. She'd even taken his dog. Then she'd given Buddy away to some guy she'd met at the dog park and had dated less than a week. Spiteful wench.

And then what had he done? Gotten sucked in by the same kind of woman.

Sure, Eva was dark were Tiffany was blonde. Eva was a minor television celebrity where Tiffany was an up-and-coming trial lawyer. Eva liked pizza. Tiffany hated it.

But overall they were the same. Both outgoing. Sparkling. Full of life.

Both full of ambition.

This won't affect our work, will it?

Thank goodness, she'd brought him back to reality.

He'd tried having a relationship with an ambitious woman. Saying it hadn't worked out was an understatement.

O'Donnells didn't pick the right partners for home and hearth.

If he needed proof, he only had to look at his immediate family. His mother and his father. He and Tiffany. His sister wouldn't give up on her hopelessly romantic dreams even after two failed marriages and one badly limping one.

Sadness swamped him. There had to be more to life than getting up, going to work and coming home to eat in front of the television while he washed clothes so he could get up and go to work again the next day.

Maybe for other people, but not for him.

"Can we turn it down?" Aaron cut through Mark's thoughts to point to the radio.

Mark wasn't oblivious to the role reversal here with the teen complaining the music was too loud.

"Fine." While he said the words out loud, they were lost in a very fine guitar riff. Mark held his hand over the volume knob until the last note faded into the engine noise of his truck before taking the sound down a couple of decibels.

"Got homework?" He fell back into the responsible adult role expected of him.

"Did it at school."

"I'll check it when we get home."

"You don't have to—"

"Want to change your answer, then?"

Mark watched Aaron slump down in his seat.

"If you want to play college ball, you've got to make the grades to keep you on the field in high school. Tutoring won't do you any good if you don't turn in your work and pass the tests."

The boy rubbed his chin.

"Hands off your face." It was an automatic response Mark should have probably swallowed this time despite Aaron's increasingly severe acne breakouts. Some things went deeper than looks.

Mark needed to remember that about everyone in his world, not just his nephew.

"Where are you? Call me."

Eva cleared her sister-in-law's five calls, each increasing in intensity, from her cellphone before phoning her back.

As soon as Susan answered, Eva started the conversation with, "I did it."

"I've been so worried." Susan picked up on Eva's opening line. "Did what?"

"I ate pizza." Eva twirled her finger in her hair, feeling both excited and uneasy at the same time. "With a guy."

Silence.

"Susan?"

"That's good, sweetie. Real good." It sounded forced, like Susan was talking through a thick throat.

"That's not what the tone of your voice says."

"It's just—we knew this day would come. This day needed to come. But sometimes it's just so hard to remember that Chuck is never coming back." Susan sniffed. "What kind of accountability partner am I? I'm supposed to be encouraging you. And I *am* proud of you. Just sometimes it's so hard to let go and go on."

Eva had been saying that same thing for almost two years. Tonight, though, the tightness in her chest, the heaviness in her heart wasn't quite so painful.

Eva swallowed hard before she could say, "I think Chuck would be okay with it."

"I know he would. He would be so happy for you." Susan noisily blew her nose. "So tell me about your date."

"It wasn't a date." Eva rubbed her finger across her lip, feeling the buzz as if Mark had just kissed her. "It was just pizza. With a co-worker who happens to be male."

"This male, is he cute?"

"Cute?" The image of Mark came to her, the masculinity that scored his face, the height and breadth of his body, the twinkle in his eyes, the hint of a dimple in his smile.

"Cute might not be the word."

Handsome. Stunning. Breathtaking. The superlatives could go on all night.

"So who is this co-worker?"

"Remember the E.R. doctor I told you about who would be joining the show?"

"Mark O'Donnell? You're talking about Mark O'Donnell?"

"Yes, Mark O'Donnell."

"Honey, I caught him on the DVR after you told me he'd guest hosted with you. You're right. Cute doesn't cover it. If I weren't already married, I would have to arm wrestle you for him—assuming he'd want a short, dumpy blonde with a ten-year-old and two toddlers hanging off her arms."

Eva had to laugh at the picture Susan painted of herself. It was quite accurate and her husband, who happened to be Eva's brother, adored her for all she was.

Eva wanted that again. That adoration. And maybe even the children. Maybe someday.

Maybe Mark? Her imagination jumped way ahead of reality. It hadn't even been a date. Just pizza.

"We work together. Nothing more. It was more of a get-acquainted kind of thing."

Only, instead of a professional handshake, they'd parted with a kiss. A kiss that made her lips burn even now.

"That's not what this sounds like. I haven't heard so much energy in your voice since—"

"It's not the guy. It's the timing. And it's no big deal. Just

two co-workers hanging out together." But Eva couldn't separate one from the other.

"Maybe." Susan echoed her doubt. "It looked like you had
good chemistry on the screen."

"The magic of television." *And of pizza. And of moonlight.*
Eva shook off her fanciful feelings.

Over the phone line she could hear one of her nieces starting to cry, that sleepy whine that wouldn't stop until Susan
gave her the attention she needed.

"Hon, I've got to go."

"I hear."

"So call me tomorrow. I want to hear more."

"Nothing more to say."

"Tomorrow. After your taping." Susan put both love and
steel in her voice. It was that steel that had kept Eva from falling apart when Chuck had died. And that love that had lent
her the strength to keep breathing through it. Susan had been
there for her every step of the way, even though she had been
doing her own grieving. Chuck had always been like a big
brother to Susan and his death had hit her very hard.

Susan had reminded Eva that she'd given her the same support through those difficult early years of marriage to Ricky.

That's what family did.

"Right. Tomorrow, after the taping. Talk to you then."

Eva hung up, looked around her apartment, which she had
manically repainted chocolate brown in the weeks following
the funeral, and decided to repaint. Instead of feeling safe
and cozy, the dark color now felt like a claustrophobic cave.

Her cave time was over.

She would pick up a few gallons of paint tomorrow after
she did her interviews at the high school. Time to brighten
up her world.

She'd painted at least once every six months since she and
Chuck had married. Chuck had always groaned, but he'd al-

ways gone along with the change, as long as he hadn't had to do it.

He'd hated painting. Too tedious, especially trimming round the windows.

He'd painted his world in broader strokes.

She studied the photo of Chuck on her mantel as she had done at least once a day since he'd been gone. He looked out at her with that big goofy grin of his. He'd always kept her honest even when she'd wanted to spin things.

It had been his honesty that had made the street gangs respect him even if they hadn't always obeyed him. He'd been one of the best for persuading them to keep their uneasy peace within their own ranks as well as with outside gangs.

But his negotiations had failed when he'd needed them most.

His only fault had been his inability to see that she could handle herself. She blamed part of that on their age difference. At eight years her senior, Chuck had taken on a paternal role on occasion. He'd had a strong need to protect her even when she could do the job herself.

And it had gotten him killed.

As she had so many times since his death, Eva felt his warmth on her back, comforting her. If she turned fast enough, could she see him there?

She murmured aloud, "I've got your back, babe. And your front. And all parts in between."

That's what he'd always said to her. What would he say now?

Time to let go and live again.

She heard him as clearly as she felt him.

"I'm trying."

It's okay that it's more than pizza.

Her body needed air. She drew in a deep breath and blew it out again.

And he was gone.

But this time the warmth didn't fade away when he did. Instead, Eva felt the beginnings of her own inner fire flicker as it tried to take hold.

She changed from her work clothes into an old T-shirt Chuck had worn during his academy days.

Instead of crawling into her big, cold bed, she flipped on her laptop.

For the first time in two years Eva pulled up the substance-abuse site and searched for information.

Signs of steroid abuse.

She researched, catching up with the newest studies, committing to memory the talking points when interviewing a steroid abuser and feeling that old spark come to life at the thought of helping people to stop hurting and start putting their lives back together.

This was what she was made for. Could she do it?

It wasn't a decision she had to make tomorrow—she glanced at the clock, after midnight—or rather today.

Going back into practice wasn't a decision she ever had to make. She could keep on doing what she was doing, what she was good at and what she enjoyed. It might not be her dream job, but it was a good job.

Her show helped multitudes of people. She had the fan mail to prove it. She only had to recall the woman at the pizza parlor to see how vital her new job was.

As the clock showed she was well on her way into tomorrow and her eyes started to sting, she shut down her laptop, exhausted enough to sleep.

Climbing into bed, she searched for the remembered feeling of Chuck next to her. It was getting harder and harder to remember that feeling.

She stacked pillows against her back and hugged another one, doing what she could to create a sense of pseudo-security.

Mark had the potential to change her world in a big way. Was that what she wanted?

She would think about it tomorrow.

Tomorrow. There would always be a tomorrow.

Except when there wasn't.

Eva surveyed the group of a dozen teens arranged on the bleachers in front of her. They watched themselves on the monitors, either boldly posturing or shyly glancing according to their natures.

"Ready?" she asked Mark, unable to squelch the bubble of resentment floating in her stomach. This segment was her bribe to play nicely. Therefore, this should have been her interview and her interview alone.

"Ready," he answered, gesturing for her to precede him as if he was in charge.

To do anything other than smile graciously would be petty and she had outgrown pettiness a dozen years ago.

As she took her seat, the teens started to whisper and squirm. Not the relaxed attitude she wanted for this frank discussion.

She wanted to put them at ease but she needed to get the preliminaries out of the way first.

"Thank you for coming," she said over their chatter.

They finished up their conversations then gave her their attention.

Meeting the eyes of each of them, she loosely clasped her hands and let them fall into her lap. "Full disclosure. Anything you say here may be shown to the entire world. Those of you who are over eighteen have signed waivers to that effect. Those of you under eighteen have turned in waivers with a parent's or guardian's signature. I intend to get into a very heavy discussion. I will tell the entire truth and I expect that from you, too. Do any of you want to change your mind now?"

Mark gave a pointed look at his nephew. Mark hadn't wanted Aaron participating in this interview, hadn't wanted to sign the waiver, but in the end Aaron had won out.

Eva was sure it had something to do with the little cheerleader she recognized from the pizza parlor snuggled up next to the big teen.

Aaron studiously avoided making eye contact with his uncle.

If anyone had wanted to back out, peer pressure kept them from speaking up. This interview would take special handling to make it real but to keep it within the realm of public airing. Waivers or not, she would never expose anything that these teens wouldn't want made public.

It was a personal barrier most reporters wouldn't put in their own paths.

"I'll stay around for questions off camera at the end of the interview." Maybe she wasn't cut out for hard-hitting journalism after all.

Eva squashed that thought as she gave her interviewees a reassuring smile.

"Let's get started." She picked up the cup of hot tea one of the gaffers had left for her and took a sip. Another ploy to put the teens at ease. Speaking into the camera, she said, "Welcome to this special segment of *Ask the Doc*. I'm Dr. Eva Veracruz and this is Dr. Mark O'Donnell. We're with a group of teen athletes from various schools across the city to ask some tough questions.

"How many of you think some professional athletes take drugs to enhance their performance?"

All hands went up.

"What drugs to you think they take?"

The teens called out.

"Speed."

"Weight-loss pills."

"Steroids."

All of them nodded. "Yeah, steroids."

"Juice."

"'Roids."

They used the most common street names for anabolic steroids.

Eva wanted to kick Mark as he furrowed his brow at the quick and easy way the teens answered. He worked in E.R. Surely he knew the worldliness of today's teens?

Or was it that he knew many of these particular teens and had thought their expensive school protected them from that side of life?

In Eva's experience, no economic stratum was immune. The only difference between wealthy and poor areas was the more expensive the school, the more expensive the drugs.

As if Mark heard her unspoken thoughts, he cleared his brow and replaced his expression of disapproval with one of interest instead.

"Why do athletes take these drugs?"

"To enhance their performance. More endurance," said one of the girls Eva recognized from her own alma mater.

"To get bigger, faster," the cheerleader next to Aaron added. As tiny as she was, Eva was fairly certain this girl had never done steroids. In fact, her small size worried Eva. She would try to keep an eye on the girl.

As outspoken as Mark's nephew usually was, he was surprisingly quiet today.

Eva made her voice casual and nonjudgmental. "Do you think high-school athletes take steroids?"

All heads nodded.

Mark might have thought that one or two of these kids might know someone who injected themselves, but they all did? Even the kids in his nephew's school?

Mark started to frown until Eva "accidentally" bumped

him with her cup of tea. Recalling his role, he wiped his expression from his face, hiding his shock.

Sure, he saw kids in the E.R. with drug problems, but those were usually mood-altering drugs, hard drugs, like meth or ecstasy.

He cleared his throat, conscious of the index cards he held in his hand that gave a brief bio of each athlete. "So what do steroids do?"

A football player from a school across town said, "You can eat all you want without getting fat."

"And you can build muscle fast, even if you don't work out much," another boy said. His card said he was on a wrestling team.

"They give you confidence," a girl he recognized from the swim team added.

Mark nodded, accepting their statements. All that was true. But there were the downsides.

"What are the side effects?"

The teens looked at each other. Half seemed not to know. The other half seemed to want to deny any side effects.

Eva leaned forward, gracefully taking the conversation back at the right time. It was as if she was the yin to his yang—at least when it came to television. How would she be when she wasn't in front of a camera?

One of Mark's strongest fantasies surfaced, a fantasy he'd never gotten to indulge in. Would Eva—?

Her no-nonsense voice cut through his daydreams.

"Steroids in teens can stunt growth."

Mark watched each students' reactions as most looked unconcerned but a few looked worried. This wasn't supposed to be a witch hunt to uncover drug use, but he couldn't help being concerned.

Aaron stared up into the rafters, his attention drifting off. Mark hoped the cameraman didn't do a close-up on his nephew while Aaron was so obviously off in his own little world.

With Mark's own very recent side trip into dream world, he couldn't fault his nephew. He just hoped Aaron's daydreams were a lot more innocent than his uncle's.

Eva gave the hand signal that called the camera's focus back to her. "Other side effects can be jaundice, which makes your skin yellow, fluid retention, which makes you look puffy, and a decrease in LDL, which you can't see but is bad for your circulatory system.

"Anyone know any other side effects?" Discreetly, Eva directed the cameras to the teens.

The little cheerleader called out, "Acne."

Next to her, Aaron gave her a deep scowl, probably due to his own blemished skin. Mark wanted to smooth over the symptom by pointing out that some acne in teens was common and the propensity was generally inherited. But Aaron would become embarrassed if he thought Mark was trying to single him out to defend him.

The boy was so sensitive about everything concerning his body. At Aaron's age, Mark remembered being self-absorbed, but not so emotional. But, then, memories did tend to replay in a kinder, gentler way as the years went by.

Eva gave the girl an encouraging nod. "Did you know there are also side effects that are specific to girls and to boys?"

Mark gave Eva kudos. Her statement piqued the interest of all the teens, even his drifting nephew.

At Eva's nod, Mark supplied the answers for the boys.

"Guys, anabolic steroids can cause infertility and a higher risk of prostate cancer." While these things should alarm the teens, Mark knew they wouldn't. Kids this age didn't worry much about the future.

"But that's not all." He set them up for the effects that would hit their vanity. "When teen boys use steroids, they can expect to see shrinking of testicles, baldness and the development of breasts. These changes are not reversible even when steroid abuse is stopped."

Every male in the gym, including the cameramen, twitched as they thought about the ramifications of steroid abuse. Even Aaron came out of his fog and focused on Mark's words.

"And, girls, you've got your own set of problems," Eva added on cue. "You can expect facial hair, male-pattern baldness, changes to or a complete stop of your menstrual cycle and a permanently deeper voice."

Noting they were out of time, Eva did the wrap-up on the effects of steroid abuse. "Steroids can give you a certain sense of well-being, but they can send you on a mood-swing binge just as easily. A steroid user can experience irrational and uncontrollable anger with little or no provocation. These 'roid rages can end up in physical confrontations that are dangerous for anyone around the steroid user as he or she spins out of control. Withdrawal from steroids can be both physical and mental, including a deep depression that can require hospitalization."

Eva looked into the camera. "If you use steroids, or you suspect a friend is using steroids, ask for help to quit. The number to call is on your screen and will be on *Ask the Doc's* website as well."

The field producer called out, "That's a wrap."

Mark touched Eva on the arm to get her attention, and got a shock to his system as well. How could a simple touch set up such shock waves?

Eva gave him her attention. "You did well today. Better than I expected."

Better than expected? What was that supposed to mean? What had she expected from him? Mark glanced down at his watch he'd started to wear because of her, suddenly realizing how late the interview had run. "I've got to get to work."

"Okay. See you tomorrow on set."

As teens surrounded Eva to ask more questions, Mark walked toward his truck, reluctance in each step. That he wanted to stay with her surprised him.

And worried him.

A few days later, he was still telling himself that Eva was not for him. He knew that with his head. So why did his mind keep drifting to memories of her in that red dress, that cleavage daring him to look? Or at the pizza place, with those lips begging to be kissed?

Strictly business, O'Donnell, he said to himself as he put his truck into park.

He had to admit that when it came to her business, Eva knew what she was doing. The stories were well researched and excellently laid out by the time it was his turn to be camera-ready. Eva focused the story, supervised the graphics and took care of the voice-over copy.

He just showed up where assigned, smiled at the little red light on the camera and followed her lead.

He'd overslept. But, then, his shift had run hours long. Monday nights were supposed to be easy, but last night had been anything but. Apparently, rival gangs had been involved in some kind of confrontation. Dispatch had followed police orders and shipped the injured to different hospitals.

The E.R. had been tense, with police standing guard everywhere and the threat of a rival member bursting in at any moment to finish what he had started.

It was one of the risks Mark took, working in one of the inner city clinics. Most days he could tell you the reward was in the diversity of cases he saw. But after last night's edginess he couldn't honestly say the risks were worth it.

He'd taken time to run home, take a shower and change clothes so he was running late. He hoped the crew understood.

Mark checked in with the crew of *Ask the Doc* who were setting up their cameras on the football field. But today wasn't about the football players. It was all about the cheerleaders.

Since Eva called the shots, she had decided to give equal time to girls' sports and boys' sports. Mark had to admit that he didn't know much about cheerleading. He hadn't even dated a cheerleader when he'd been playing football.

His steady girlfriend had been a cute little library nerd. Everyone had said they didn't fit together, but they had. She had been his calm in the storm of teenage hormones and the ever-changing hurricane winds of his home life.

Then she had moved away. Without her anchoring personality, he'd been hell on wheels during his senior year. His father had even gotten involved, promising and threatening. All empty promises and threats, but at least he'd paid Mark a fraction of the attention Mark had craved from him.

Mark waved at Aaron, who was running laps, but the boy didn't wave back. Was he being ignored as too old and uncool to acknowledge or had Aaron really not seen him? Either way was okay, as long as Aaron knew Mark would be there whenever the boy needed him.

So many people, from his peers to adults, had been there for him as he'd been growing up. How did kids make it without being surrounded by such strong influences?

Who had influenced Eva? Who had been her support system? Who had she leaned on?

The memory of the way her body had felt against his when he'd kissed her made him wish she'd lean on him again—at least physically.

But she wanted to keep things strictly business. Fine. He would keep it strictly business. No sense in encouraging a closeness he didn't even want with her. He might not ever be ready for that kind of closeness again. Nothing wrong with being single the rest of his life. *Right?*

* * *

Eva watched the cheerleaders do their round-offs and back handsprings across the mat in the gym as they psyched themselves for setting up their pyramid.

"Go, Gators!" echoed to the rafters as they clapped and shouted.

Their mascot, a freshman girl sweating in her alligator costume, yelled out, "Hey, Doc! My mom says to tell you she loves your show."

"Always nice to hear."

And if their ratings didn't improve, she'd soon stop hearing it. The producers had really pinned a lot of hope on Mark's macho magnetism getting the middle-aged female crowd to tune in.

Eva had already decided she would be dusting off her résumé. Keeping it updated was the smart thing to do.

She turned her attention back to the cheerleaders. She recognized the slight cheerleader from the last recording. The girl seemed to be having trouble gaining any height in jumps.

Without meaning to, Eva realized she was analyzing the girl's health.

The girl was at least ten, maybe even fifteen pounds underweight. But that happened sometimes in puberty. Some girls grew taller faster than they could put on weight.

The girl's hair was stringy and lank. Not an indicator of anything by itself. Eva pushed her own overgrown mop out of her face. Not everyone was born with thick hair.

When she wasn't practicing, the girl continually bounced and rubbed her arms as if she were cold.

It was September in New Orleans. No one in this town had been cold in months.

Anorexia?

Mark walked up behind her. Funny how she knew it was

him without even turning around. Funny how she got shivers when he stood this close to her. Funny how she liked it.

She felt edgy, waiting, anticipating. *Foolish.*

Crushes were for teenagers.

But that kiss at the pizza parlor had been all grown up.

She turned to him. "Hi."

"Hi." His eyes looked heavy, like he'd just woken up. His hair was damp. He smelled of soap and man.

"Do you know that girl?" Eva looked in the direction of the cheerleader who was preparing to be thrown to the top of the pyramid.

Mark studied the girl. "No, I don't. I've seen her around Aaron but he hasn't introduced me to her yet."

The head cheerleader called off the count and yelled, "Up."

Precariously, the girl found her footing on the hands of the lower tier of the human tower. She balanced then raised her hands high. "Does she look unhealthy to you? Too thin maybe?"

Mark gave a noncommittal shrug. "Maybe."

Eva winced at the height of the two-high pyramid. Such risks for their sport. But that's what made it a sport, she guessed. The thrill of achievement.

She wasn't so far past those years that she didn't remember it.

As head cheerleader, she had organized the girls to beg their sponsor to build to two and a half high, but the stalwart woman had wisely refused.

She also remembered that they had all thought they were invincible back then. Bad things happened to other people, never them.

The coach called out, "Nice, Sharona. Next time, we'll try for the handstand, okay?"

Handstand? Eva didn't want to be around to watch that one. Observing this practice session was nerve-racking enough.

"So, were you ever a cheerleader?"

"Yes, all through junior high and my freshman year in high school, before I fell in love with basketball. But I was always in the base holding up everyone else."

"Solid. Dependable. Strong. It says a lot about you."

"Heavy and tall is what it says about me." She nodded towards the girl, who was getting ready for her dismount. Two of the male cheerleaders were standing by as spotters ready to catch her if she fell. "I could never be the flyer, even if I were smaller and lighter."

"Afraid of heights?"

"Trust issues." Eva surprised herself by admitting to that.

"Still have those issues?"

She crossed her arms, feeling exposed, pulling back. "That was then. This is now."

"You didn't answer the question, Doctor."

"Let's just say I would be very uncomfortable standing on the shoulders of other people."

She had stood on Chuck's shoulders. Even when she'd wanted off, he had kept her up there, like a statue on a pedestal. If only he had backed off and let her do her job, he would still be alive today.

She'd thought she was over the anger. Anger was step two of the five steps of grief. Why did she keep coming back to it? Why couldn't she let it go?

"I've got really broad shoulders." The smile he sent her suggested a relationship but what kind? Friendship? Lovers? Co-workers who happened to have good synchronicity?

She glanced down at her bare toes—she'd left her heels at the edge of the gym floor. "I've got really big feet. I've always been able to stand on them on my own." *Except when Chuck died.*

But she hadn't felt shaky in some time now. Looking back, she still felt weak for falling apart after the shooting, no matter how often Susan insisted she was normal. A normal reaction to an abnormal situation.

Mark's eyes lost the glint that asked for more than she could give. He glanced at his new watch. "The camera crew sent me to get you. They probably think we've both gotten lost now."

"Okay." Eva walked towards her shoes, missing the inches that put her on a more equal footing with Mark

Before she left the gym, she gave one last look at the girl, Sharona. What should she do? Approach the girl's coach? Observe for a while longer? Let it go?

She never used to be so indecisive. Another sign of the weakness she'd developed with the loss of Chuck.

Mark must have sensed her hesitancy. "I'll ask her coach if there has been any noticeable weight loss. And I'll pay better attention when she's hanging around Aaron and their friends."

"Thank you." Like a weight, the responsibility she felt toward Sharona lightened. If her indecision meant she failed to do her duty, Mark would take care of the girl. He would be *her* spotter. Catch her when she fell.

And she would let him. For the sake of the girl.

Mark narrowed his eyes as he put the pieces together. Trust issues. The way she often twisted a non-existent ring on her finger, like she had as she'd worried over Sharona's welfare. The whispers he'd overheard from a crew member about Eva's *husband.*

He'd assumed she was divorced. They'd kissed.

She wasn't that type, he was sure of it. She wouldn't betray her husband that way, right? But, then, he'd thought his ex hadn't been that way either.

His confidence in his ability to judge women had been shot out from under him during the long months of discovery preceding his divorce.

As he followed Eva off the court, he reached out for her then let his hand fall. What if she was—?

"Eva, your official bio says single. That's not hype, is it? Are you married?"

She stopped so fast, he ran into the back of her.

When he put his hands on her waist to steady her, she pulled back and his heart sank.

He'd kissed her and had fantasies of doing more. Much more.

He wiped his mouth with the back of his hand. He would never do that to another guy. Thanks to his ex, he knew how it felt to be that other guy.

Her face had drained of all color and her white teeth had bitten into her blood-red-painted bottom lip.

"Married?" She twirled the non-existent ring on her finger once again. "No, I—"

"No explanations, please. Yes or no will do."

"I kissed you. How could you think that?"

"That sounds like a stall tactic to me." His stomach was roiling as he guessed why she must be stalling. What excuse would she give him? "Still waiting. Yes or no?"

"No." Her answer came on a breath of expelled air, as if she'd used all she had to push the word out of herself. She hung her head. "Not any more."

Sympathy swamped him. "Divorce is tough."

She thought about shrugging in agreement, letting the remark pass as she usually did. Instead she said the first response that popped into her head. "So is death.

"I'm…" her mouth worked as if she were trying to pronounce a complicated foreign word "…widowed."

Mark's blue-green eyes darkened as he looked away. "I'm sorry."

"Thank you."

The pain in her voice struck deep into his gut.

"I'm sorry," he repeated. The words weren't enough. They didn't cover his apology for misjudging her for something she hadn't done, or his sympathy for the loss of her husband or his regret that he'd caused her pain by demanding an answer from her. But it's all he had.

"It's all right." With sad eyes, she gave him a forgiving smile then covered his hand with hers, trying to give him comfort when he should be comforting her. "I've just never said that out loud before."

"How long have you been a widow?" The compassion in his voice was so raw, so sincere and so understanding that she wondered about his own losses.

"Two years. I'm over the worst of it, I think, but sometimes it catches me off guard." She shifted, feeling her world steady under her. "He wouldn't want me to grieve forever."

"Wise man."

"No. Not wise at all. But very brave." Some time during the last two years Eva's pain and anger had turned to bittersweet nostalgia. It's what Chuck would have wanted.

"I'm sure he was a great guy."

"He was." She reached up, her palm cool on his cheek. "I think he would have liked you."

She dropped her hand and stood firmly on those two feet she was so proud of. "But that doesn't really matter. What matters is that I like you."

CHAPTER FIVE

WHAT MATTERS IS that I like you.

Mark had been thinking about those words ever since Eva had uttered them before walking away from him.

Like. As in co-worker? Friend? Potential lover?

What did he mean to Eva? And what did she mean to him?

Like was too simple a word to describe the reactions she induced in him.

She was the widow of a brave man. How could he compete with the ghost of a hero?

Her kind of baggage wasn't what he needed in his life right now.

Just what do you need? his inner voice asked.

Unsuccessfully, he tried to push away the name Eva that kept popping up in his head.

Her eyes had gone serious when she'd talked of her late husband. Serious and something else. Something beyond sadness. Something much more nebulous. Wistfulness?

Ghosts made for an awkward ménage à trois.

But living, breathing Eva haunted him.

After a full week of working together, Mark was in total sync with Eva. Everyone on set agreed that the way they finished each other's sentences was uncanny.

Very personally and privately Mark thought the way her touch could send energy through him was uncanny.

The harder he tried to keep a professional distance, the closer Eva inched her way into his head.

She was so smart she challenged his own thinking, making him look at the world in a different way, a bigger way. She had a wicked sense of humor that could defuse any on-set tension. She had a way of explaining even the most complicated medical matter so anyone could understand.

And she seemed to genuinely like him.

How could he keep his distance from a woman like that?

And then there was that kiss. It lay between them like a golden egg, its existence shining bright but barely believable, a moment out of time waiting to be acknowledged.

So each day, after finishing up in E.R., he could barely make himself sleep before he rushed off to meet with Eva for that day's shooting.

And her smile always, always made him feel like she'd been waiting just for him.

So, as he drove towards today's assignment, Mark's pulse began to race in anticipation.

Eva worried about Mark.

Between his hospital work and his television work, his days were certainly being filled to the brim but he hadn't complained that she'd heard of.

The work was energizing for Eva.

She had thought being cut back to only three days on air would give her more personal time. Instead, she had less.

Field work took a lot more hours to produce than studio work. But it also gave her great pleasure—almost as much pleasure as seeing Mark each afternoon as they interviewed and filmed for the upcoming shows.

Today Eva visited her own alma mater high school.

They were doing some pre-taping for a segment that would air next week on how schools with limited funds could keep their athletes safe while staying competitive. She and her staff had really had to dig into the research to find affordable protective equipment, but she was proud of the list they had compiled.

Then she and Mark would play that one-on-one basketball game he'd promised her. She had worked it around to raise money for the school's athletic department.

With mega-publicity, the station had sold over three hundred tickets to the game, with all profits to be donated to the school. Of course, they were reaping the benefits as well in all the publicity they were generating.

Eva hoped that would translate into viewing figures. It seemed the competing television station continued to win the ratings war for every show except the recent ones she'd shared with Mark.

As her agent sadly said, this was not a good thing.

She and her crew did some initial filming, including highlighting the championship basketball trophies her team had won three out of the four years she had played. They took extra delight in taking artistic shots of her individual trophies for team high scorer those three years.

Then she went into the locker room to change. So many memories.

This was where she'd discussed boys, the right ones and the wrong ones. It was also where she and her girlfriends had discussed drugs and unprotected sex and who had dropped out of school before they'd earned their diplomas.

The dropout rate at Mark's alma mater was almost zilch. Her school's was close to forty percent some years.

They were from two different worlds.

Why was she so attracted to him?

And the big question she'd been pondering all week was what was she going to do about it?

She stripped off her dress and heels and donned gym shorts and gym shoes.

What would Mark think of her stripped-down look?

Stripped down. All kinds of meanings there.

She looked forward to seeing *his* stripped-down look both on and off the court.

Doubling up on sports bras made breathing barely manageable but bouncing out of the question.

She stood on tiptoe to get a better full-length view in the short mirrors mounted over the row of sinks.

Her thighs were full, well muscled and very strong. She'd turned more than one guy's head, if he liked her kind of look. If he didn't, there was nothing she could do about it.

She would remember that when Mark saw her in shorts. If he didn't like what he saw, there was nothing she could do about it.

If self-esteem issues were hitting her now, at her present age, how much worse was it for the teens who stared into these cloudy mirrors, wondering about the boys who awaited them just outside the locker room doors?

Hairbrush in hand, she wrestled her hair into a rubber band. The big, frizzy ponytail took her back several years, undoing all the sophistication she'd worked so hard for.

But if outward appearances were her only signs of maturation, she really hadn't grown up much, had she?

Sweating was a certainty in the un-air-conditioned gym. With a big sigh she washed off her makeup. Better bare faced than streaked with a gloppy combination of foundation, blush and mascara running from eye to chin.

"Welcome back to your terrible teens, Eva," she told herself in the mirror. Her reflection smirked back at her.

She could definitely still see teen Eva behind the eyes of

adult Eva. At least she didn't do the dumb things she'd done back then.

Those teen years had been pretty terrible. And she hadn't had a benevolent uncle to bail her out like Aaron had. Only a very strict grandmother who hadn't had the funds to fix whatever trouble Eva had got into. Thankfully, it had never been as bad as Aaron's.

But Ricky's had been that bad.

Her brother was the poster boy for bad turned good. That wouldn't have happened without a lot of outside help.

If only Mark would accept outside help for Aaron, Eva would do her best to turn him around, too.

No matter what side of town the kids came from, trouble would put them in the same cells in the same detention centers.

Eva gave her unpolished self one last look in the mirror, held her head high, faking self-confidence just like she'd done in high school, and headed to the basketball court to face off against the only man in the whole city she wanted to impress.

Mark looked around at the packed gym. Everyone had paid to celebrate the celebrity their home-grown girl had become.

He clearly did not have the crowd on his side.

He bounced the basketball a couple of times. This wasn't really his game. Sure, he'd shot a few hoops, but only when there hadn't been a football to throw around. So he wouldn't have to hold back too badly to keep from showing Eva up.

She said she'd played, but she was such a girly girl he found that hard to imagine.

What he could imagine was that girly-girl body under his very testosterone-laden touch.

He put the reins on that image. He had a job to do. Distraction at work wasn't the way to get the job done.

He hoped she didn't try to do this in her heels—or her bare

feet, which was how she'd walked onto the gym floor during cheerleader practice last week. Victory by forfeit due to injury was such an unsatisfactory way to win and it wouldn't make very good television either.

Wouldn't it be ironic for a show that emphasized proper equipment?

Shyness overtook Eva as she stood in the doorway of the gym. She was used to hiding behind her makeup, giving the world what it wanted to see. But today she was giving the world who she really was. Today she was pure Eva.

And on that note she lifted her chin, pasted on an unvarnished smile and jogged out to the middle of the court where Mark and the referee awaited her.

The cheers of the crowd put a bounce in her step. The startled look in Mark's eyes put a question in her ego.

As the referee explained the ground rules to them and to the crowd, she cast surreptitious looks his way.

His legs were long and muscled. A plus in her book. Bird legs were not her thing.

His sleeveless shirt showed off his biceps. They were well defined, almost to the point of bulging. There was no doubt his body was still benefitting from all those years of high-school sports. Did they feel as hard as they looked?

"Want to make this game a little more interesting?"

Eva grinned. "What do you have in mind?"

"I hear you're a pretty good cook. I win, you cook supper for me."

Eva had no idea where he'd heard that. She was an awful cook. "And if I win?"

"Not going to happen." He said it like he thought it was a given that she would lose.

That was it. Eva was going to win this one. "Let's just say, for the sake of equality, I tell you what I want if I win."

"Okay, tell me."

What did she want? His hands on her? His mouth on her?

"Help me paint my apartment."

"Sure." He gave her a wink. "Not going to happen, but for the sake of fairness I agree to that."

The referee asked if they wanted to free-throw for possession of the ball.

"No need," Mark answered him. "Ladies first."

Eva acknowledged his chivalry with a nod of her head. While good manners wouldn't buy him a court advantage, it certainly bought him a personal one.

"I appreciate gallantry in my gentlemen opponents." She bounced the ball once then spun it on her fingertip before dribbling it through her legs.

As surprise cleared from his eyes, approval took its place.

His eyes lingered on her legs. "You look ready to get serious about this."

She gave him a cocky wink. "I'm always serious about winning."

And the game commenced.

If anyone had asked, Eva would have told them she kept her eyes on Mark's swiveling hips to anticipate his breaks, and it would be true. But she wouldn't be able to deny that she took great pleasure in watching those hips, those legs, those hands as he bounced the ball.

And her intent study enabled her to take that basketball away from him often enough to score nine points to his eight.

While his short game was good, she had cut her teeth on this court and the support of the crowd bolstered her confidence.

This was the feeling sports gave an athlete—the feeling of confidence, of pride, of challenge, and tonight she would embrace the feeling of victory.

As she took possession of the ball, she decided to go for

the long shot. Using their modified rules, the two-point shot would give her the win.

Taking the ball out, she crouched opposite Mark, eye to eye. How to get past his defenses?

Use your talents, her coach had always told her.

She smiled, a predatory smile.

Mark didn't answer that smile. Instead, he frowned, intently waiting to pounce.

Then she played her winning move.

Very deliberately, she licked her lips.

His eyes diverted to her mouth.

She took the shot—a long shot. And watched the ball circle the rim then fall neatly through the basket.

The crowd went crazy and Eva yelled with them.

And Mark stood there, shock evident on his face as he looked from her empty hands to the scoreboard.

"How did that happen?"

She smiled into his stunned eyes. "Pre-judgment? Underestimating? Plain ol' outplayed?"

"I'm pretty sure I've never come across that last move of yours executed quite that way."

"My long shot?" she asked innocently.

"Yes, your long shot. I think it had something to do with your game face."

The crowd was now swarming the floor, their volume swelling in the acoustically inclined basketball court.

Using the noise as an excuse, he leaned in close to whisper in her ear, "Want to discuss that move over supper?"

"You owe me a paint job, remember? A dinner out would be too easy."

"There's nothing about you that's easy, Eva. You're one of the most complex women I've ever met." Mark gave her a shiver-inducing smile. "The dinner out with you would be my consolation prize. I could use some good company to soothe my ego."

"Aunt Eva, you won!" Eva's ten-year-old niece, Selma, pushed through the crowd to rush up to her. "Girls rule! Boys drool!"

Eva smiled down at her niece. "A good sport doesn't gloat."

"What's gloat?"

Eva thought about that one for a moment. She sent Mark a sideways glance. "It's when the winner doesn't make fun of the loser by saying he drools."

"So what does a good sport do when she wins?" Mark asked with a twinkle in his eyes.

Eva twinkled back. "She graciously accepts compliments."

"And dinner invitations?" Mark tried again. "In addition to the paint job, of course."

Selma glared at Mark. "Momma made us dinner, remember? She even made a winner's cake."

Eva gave Mark a reluctant shrug. "Maybe another time?"

While Eva was sure that whatever her sister-in-law had cooked for them would be wonderful, she was equally as sure that only Mark could fill that other kind of hunger that plagued her.

It was time and her gut feeling told her that Mark was the man.

Her only question was how to make it happen. It had been a while—a long while—since she'd needed to vamp a man.

CHAPTER SIX

EVA DID AS much pre-taping as she could without Mark. It was a noble gesture. He needed his rest.

But it came at a price because she discovered she needed him.

The three days without seeing him were like three days without sunshine. How had that happened? How had he become such a central part of her day?

And what would she do when they were done with the series?

What could she do to make sure the relationship continued long after their time together on *Ask the Doc* ended?

He'd been friendly, sometimes even a little bit flirty on set, responding to her banter in kind when the cameras were recording. But ever since their flirting on the basketball court he'd kept things between them strictly professional when the cameras weren't rolling.

It seemed she would need to be the assertive one here. It wasn't a role she'd ever played before. In high school her friends had all hung out together, boys and girls. They had paired up for an occasional under-the-bleachers experience, broken up, then paired up again.

She'd met Chuck her first year out of high school and they'd become friends while she'd worked her way through college. She hadn't had time for anyone else.

Gradually, their friendship had turned to something deeper, something more binding, something the poets only dreamed about.

What was happening with her and Mark? No casual friendship with a slow build-up to something more.

Their relationship was more like immediate attraction with a slow growth of mutual respect.

Relationship. What she knew about Mark told her he wouldn't have approved of her use of that word. But, then, what she knew about him outside work could fit into a thimble.

To keep her mind off Mark after work, Eva had haunted the home-improvement stores. She'd collected swatches of paint in colors ranging from traditional white to bright red.

She'd finally settled on a pale yellow. Light and sunny but subtle enough to fade into the background. The salesman had warned her that she would need to prime over the dark chocolate color with a thick base coat then cover it with at least two coats of yellow.

This could be a long project. That was a good thing.

Relationship or not, she intended Mark to make good on his bet. If the opportunity arose, she would be ready for him this weekend.

Ready for him. In how many ways could she be ready for him?

All of them. Eva could too easily imagine them painting together, laughing together, celebrating a job well done with a glass of wine or a beer and take-out tamales from the vendor down the street.

It would be good to have life back in her apartment again.

Finally it was Friday.

Mark hadn't seen Eva since their basketball game. The producers had enough footage of him for the next several shows so he hadn't needed to show up for the camera.

Those three days seemed like two years. They had felt off somehow. Not in sync. Not right. He tried to deny it, but couldn't. Those days hadn't gone right because he hadn't had the chance to bask in Eva's smile. His attraction for her was getting totally out of control and he wasn't happy about it.

On the practical side, he'd needed the time off from the show. He'd had to attend a parent-teacher meeting for Aaron alone because his sister had decided to take a vacation.

The results of that meeting were not good. Aaron would need to get his grades up or be kicked off the team. Mark saw many hours of homework supervision in his future.

And then there was work at the hospital. The full moon always increased the activity and severity of the cases that came into the E.R. He'd needed to work extended hours all week, as had all the other E.R. doctors. He was exhausted.

Until these last days without seeing her, Mark hadn't realized how much energy he drew from Eva's enthusiasm.

As he drove to the studio, he sipped more coffee to drown his yawns.

First, the live taping of *Ask the Doc*, then to bed.

What would Eva look like in his bed? That glorious hair spread out on his pillow. That glorious body spread out on his sheets.

Enough, O'Donnell.

For the thousandth time he reminded himself that playing where he worked was not a good idea. Too much could go wrong with his professional life.

And playing with a woman who put work first was an even worse idea. Too much could go wrong with his personal life.

Then again there was her late husband, as solidly between them as if he were still alive.

Three excellent reasons. Why didn't they seem like enough?

Because they were excuses.

The real reason had nothing to do with Eva and everything to do with him.

Entering into an emotional relationship meant the beginning of the end. And the thought of ending anything with Eva made him feel incredibly sad. At least this way, by keeping everything totally professional, they *had* a relationship, even if it was a working one.

But it wasn't the connection he needed. Wanted—not needed. He didn't need anyone.

On automatic pilot, Mark parked his truck and headed into the studio, carrying his suit bag. This time he'd kept his suit hanging safely in the dry cleaner's bag in his truck, with intentions to change once he got into the studio. Unlike his first show there would be no more casual scrubs on television for him.

As he stared into the brightly lit mirror in his dressing room and tied his tie, he downed his third cup of coffee in so many hours.

Mark rubbed his hand over his face, emotional exhaustion taking as much of a toll as physical exhaustion.

After a night like last night, all the little things seemed so trivial. Part of dealing with trauma, he knew. So much life-and-death drama skewed normal perspectives.

He took a deep breath, trying to find his balance. Eva would help with that without even knowing it. He'd learned that about her, not only by watching her but by watching her crew. Things fell into place when she was around.

Always back to Eva. He was so obsessed.

Right now he was too tired to fight it. He'd have to settle for hiding it instead.

"Let's do this," he said to the mirror, calling on his last

reserves, then felt foolish as he realized Eva was standing outside his open door, about to knock.

"Rough night?" She moved to stand just inside the doorway, revealing an electric-blue dress and heels so high they had to be stressing every bone in her feet but made her legs look incredibly sexy.

"It shows?" He clenched his eyes in a hard blink before focusing again on those shoes. It was better than inspecting her breasts. And that sunny smile only reminded him how tired he was.

His ex-wife had worn impractical heels. She'd always said they projected an image of power. But he'd rubbed her feet enough to know the torture shoes like those caused. All for illusion.

Eva gave him a sympathetic smile. "Full moon means full wards, right?"

"I'm afraid so." He rubbed his eyes with the backs of his fists as if he could rub away all he'd seen last night. Instead, that brief lapse of sight only made the images more detailed in his mind.

"Want to tell me about it?"

"So you can use it on the show?" That came out sharper than Mark had intended. "Sorry. It's just that…"

"It's just that…?"

"Yeah. Rough night." He rubbed his hand across his face, not helping the stress lines that the bright set lights would emphasize.

He should have stopped right there. He knew from experience that unburdening himself would only cause problems with those not initiated into the nastier side of New Orleans nightlife.

But when Eva propped herself against the doorjamb and waited, looking like she truly wanted to understand, he couldn't find the strength to stop the pain that spilled out.

His voice cracked as he asked, more the universe than Eva, "How can kids be so stupid?"

"What happened?"

"Underage drinking and driving. An overloaded car full of kids. We couldn't even keep them responsive long enough to notify their parents and give them a chance to say good-bye. Instead, those parents got early-morning knocks on their doors. We could only save one. And she's on the ragged edge."

Eva clenched and unclenched her hands while sympathetic tears welled. "My husband worked for the New Orleans Police Department. He used to have to make those visits. They tore him apart."

Mark turned away, not able to face the tragedy in her eyes. "You'd think, after all these years, it would get easier."

She walked towards him and put a hand on his shoulder. He looked at their reflections in the mirror, not really seeing either or them.

"After the teenagers there was a knifing and then a domestic fight." He reached deep, trying to gather the last shreds of inner strength. "And just when I think I can't do this any more, I get to witness a miracle."

He handed her a tissue. "You don't want to have to redo your makeup."

"Thanks." She dabbed under her eyes. "The miracle?"

"The baby was crowning as the taxi pulled into E.R. We didn't even have time to wheel the mother up to Maternity. The cord was wrapped around his neck, but I worked it free before it damaged him." Mark drew in a deep breath and took heart that Eva was still listening. "That little boy stopped crying, wrapped his fingers around my thumb, and looked up at me as if he could really focus on me. And I felt…"

"Felt what, Mark?"

"I felt… This sounds silly, I guess, but I felt hope. That maybe this little guy would do something someday that would make the world a better place. And I got the privilege of helping him start out."

Eva forgot to dab and a dark-streaked tear tracked down her cheek.

Quick footsteps drew nearer to the dressing room and the producer stuck his head in the door.

"You're both here. Good. Five minutes." Then he paused, and yelled down the hallway, "We need Make-up in here."

The studio's makeup artist came rushing in from Eva's dressing room. "Stop, Dr. Veracruz. Stop crying. You are ruining your eyes."

The woman glared at Mark as if it was all his fault. And it was.

The makeup artist did something with a sponge and Eva looked as if she'd never shed a tear in her life.

"Now for you, Dr. O'Donnell. Look at those dark circles." She pointed the sponge at Eva. "You were going to call me in if he needed a touch-up."

"I got distracted."

The woman came over to wrap a paper collar round Mark's neck. Instinctively, Mark drew away.

Eva took a step to stand between his chair and the makeup artist. "Leave him just like he is."

"But that face. Those eyes."

"He's earned the right to look like he does today." She turned to her producer. "You want this to be real, right, Phil?"

"Yes, but—"

"Then we'll tell our audience the truth. Mark has been up all night in the E.R. and hasn't been home to rest yet. They need to know he's the real thing."

Mark met her gaze in the mirror as they both remembered how he had accused her of being a pretend doctor. And right now, as she stood there in her silk dress and heels, staring the reality of medicine in the face, she felt like a fake.

When she'd given up practicing medicine, should she have given up the privilege of calling herself a doctor, too?

"But…" Phil swiveled between her, Mark and the makeup artist.

"Give me some artistic license on this, Phil." She gave him the smile that one of the New Orleans newspapers had said was full of more intelligence and honesty than any other on television. "Trust me."

The alarm on his watch beeped. "I don't have any other choice. We're out of time."

The intro music played and Mark followed Eva onto the live set. The audience was at full capacity today, he'd been told, but he could only see a blur of faces in the front rows. The lights blinded him to everything else.

Remembering his manners, he waited for Eva to sit, then took his place next to her.

"Good morning and welcome to *Ask the Doc*," Eva began, her voice bringing the crowd to a level of cheering usually reserved for the football stands.

Mark soaked in the much-needed energy. He could see how a person could get use to this.

"As you know, on Fridays we have two doctors in the house. Dr. O'Donnell joins us straight from the E.R., where he has been working the night shift." She graciously waved her hand towards Mark while the camera followed her direction.

Mark gave the camera a tight smile. "Thank you, Dr. Veracruz."

Then he dropped the smile and looked straight at the blinking red light. "Last night was a rough one in the E.R. with accidents that should have never happened." He swallowed. "Parents, teens think they are invincible, especially when they drink. They don't understand their own mortality. Teach them, tell them, show them. Don't let your kids drink and drive."

Mark didn't know why he'd said that. If Eva had done it, he might have accused her of exploiting a tragic situation. But sitting there, he realized if he could just say it with the right words in the right way, he could reach a lot of people and he just might save a life. He remembered the woman from the pizza place.

The power of television.

Now he watched Eva trying to turn his dramatic statement into an upbeat segue about their sponsor, a popular sports drink provider that had bought advertising time on the show.

Instead of turning the attitude with one of her hundred-watt smiles, she leaned forward, solemnity in every line of her face. "All you adults who are responsible for teens, whether you are a mom or dad or grandparent or aunt or uncle or older sibling—be the parent. Not the best friend. Not the provider of goods and services, but the stalwart guide for your teen. It's a demanding job. But the future rewards are worth it."

Now came the smile as she leaned back and relaxed. He could feel the audience take a deep, calming breath with her. She was that good.

"And for all of you who are raising your teens the right way, kudos to you. We know it's the toughest job in the world."

She started clapping and the audience, of course, followed suit. She could engender such intimacy, such trust, they would jump off a cliff for her.

Mark added his own applause.

He made a mental note for after the show to say thanks to her for adding in caretakers other than parents.

He also picked up, from her darting sideways glance, that she had no transition into their show—which was totally his fault with his ad lib opening.

He gave her a cocky grin to let her know he had it under control then used the subtle hand gesture he'd seen her use to get the cameraman's attention.

20% OFF*

with code
THANKSJUN

Visit www.millsandboon.co.uk
today to get this exclusive offer!

Ordering online is easy:

- 1000s of stories converted to eBook
- Big savings on titles you may have missed in store

Visit today and enter the code **THANKSJUN** at the checkout today to receive **20% OFF** your next purchase of books and eBooks*. You could be settling down with your favourite authors in no time!

MILL
BOO

JUN1

"It takes a village. Here's to the teachers, the neighbors and the coaches who are instrumental in your teen's life. Adding a very personal thank you to my high-school football coach, Randy Carter, who will probably never realize what a huge positive influence he was in my life.

"Which brings us to today's show—the influence of sports in our teens' lives. Our thanks to our sponsors for giving us drinks to take home to our thirsty teens, and for the rest of our active households, too. We'll be back right after this message from them."

Thanks to Eva, the show was packed full of good information on nutrition and rest requirements for teen athletes. The graphics were easy to follow and the tips were easy to remember. Mark had had no idea that teen girls needed a minimum of two thousand two hundred calories a day.

He'd bet his All-State letter jacket patch that the cheerleader who Eva was worried about, Sharona, never ate that much in a day.

He'd had a call in to the high-school counselor to discuss having a conference with Sharona's parents and her coach about her rapid weight loss over the summer but so far her parents hadn't responded.

As interesting as it was, Eva's nutrition information didn't take over all his thoughts.

Why was he fighting his attraction to Eva so hard?

She'd been the one to kiss him after all. Why couldn't he give in to physical need while keeping his emotions safe?

Other guys did it all the time, right?

But Mark never had. He'd always wanted more.

And look where that's got you, O'Donnell.

Would he make a play for Eva or not? He'd never been this indecisive about a woman before. But this wasn't just any woman. This was Eva.

Maybe he should walk away. Call it a chance not taken. *Regret playing it safe for the rest of his life.*

He felt as if he was balancing fifteen tons on each of his shoulders. Any tipping to one side or the other and he would end up crushed beneath the weight of his own worries.

He knew this would be one decision that would have serious repercussions on his life, whatever he decided.

He also knew never to make decisions when he was too tired to think straight.

Of course. His exhaustion explained his indecision. A few good, hard hours of sleep and he would know if he wanted to back down or step up.

Before he realized what was happening, Eva was delivering her closing tagline.

He found himself automatically smiling and nodding—his only responsibility in closing the show. If any of the previous cue cards had been for him, Eva had covered for him.

"Good show." Eva followed her compliment with an energy-boosting smile. "The cheerleaders have asked me to come to the game tonight. Will I see you there?"

"Absolutely. It would be bad luck to miss the first game of the season. Want me to save you a seat?"

"Save two."

Two? Mark wanted to ask. But it really wasn't his business and it certainly wasn't anything he was prepared to handle right now.

Instead, he concentrated on getting home and getting himself to bed to recover from his night shift.

He was usually good at sleeping any time, anywhere.

But today a beam of sunlight pierced the crack between his heavy curtains just as Eva's kiss pierced his memory, making him toss and turn instead of rest.

He'd finally dropped off to sleep when Aaron stuck his

head into his bedroom. "I'm riding with Sandy tonight, okay?"

Aaron had that tone in his voice, the one that sounded way too casual, the one that meant he was trying to get away with something.

Promising himself extra hours of sleep tomorrow, Mark hauled himself out of bed.

"Math homework?"

"Got it done."

"Let me see it." Mark made his way to the table where Aaron traditionally dumped his backpack. "English paper?"

"Got it done, too."

"Really?" He picked up the crumpled mess that was Aaron's math homework. He could see plenty of erasures, which meant Aaron's tutor had helped the best she could with it.

"I spent time in the library today after tutoring."

Mark glanced at the clock on the kitchen wall. It was a good cover for being late, although highly unlikely. But he had no proof to the contrary so he refrained from calling Aaron on it.

"Who typed your paper for you?" Mark had seen his nephew's painful typing skills. The kid was a wiz at texting on his phone's keyboard, but anything requiring more than two fingers left the boy angry and frustrated.

"I did."

"Let me see it." Mark sent a not-quite-nice thought in his sister's direction. She should be the one taking care of this. But she was too busy with her new husband. History repeating itself. Their mother had been the same way.

Thankfully, *he* had never needed help with his schoolwork and his coach had provided much-needed guidance when he'd stepped out of line. Mark pushed away the exhaustion that was fast playing havoc with his attitude and reminded himself he was just paying it forward.

Someday, hopefully, Aaron would do the same.

Mark scanned the paper. "Very impressive."

"Thanks."

This was going to make him late. So much for saving seats for Eva and whoever she was bringing to the game. But taking care of his pseudo-parental obligation took priority over his libido.

Libido. It seems he'd woken up knowing his answer about Eva.

Mark looked up over the top of the paper. The boy was going to try to bluff his way through this. How dumb did he think his uncle was?

"So this word *'obsequious.'* Tell me what it means."

Aaron shrugged, but his casual gesture didn't erase the defiance he showed in the thrust of his jaw. "I forgot. I knew it when I wrote the paper, though."

"How about this word, *'sequential'*?"

"I looked them up in that dinosaur word book."

Dinosaur word book? Mark had to think about that one. "What book would that be, Aaron?"

"You know, the one that sounds like a tyrannosaurus."

"The thesaurus?"

"Yeah, that's the one."

Good old thesaurus rex. Mark bit the inside of his cheek to keep from laughing. Instead of seeing the belligerent seventeen-year-old in front of him, Mark was remembering the funny little three-year-old Aaron used to be who'd demanded ships for lunch instead of chips.

"I'm not even going to ask the question when I already know the answer. I hope this paper set your savings account back a hefty amount of money." Mark tore it up as Aaron's face turned bright red and his eyes flashed. But those angry eyes didn't intimidate Mark like they did the boy's mother.

"Consider this your last night of freedom and you're only

getting tonight because you finished your math homework. Tomorrow you write your paper. You'll be grounded until the paper is done."

Aaron balled his fists. This past summer he'd knocked a hole through his mother's wall—that had been the last she'd been able to take of his behavior.

Mark widened his stance the same way he faced down gang members and thugs in the E.R. He worked hard to keep his expression firm while his stomach sank. He'd never thought he would have to confront his own nephew this way.

"Don't do it, Aaron."

He must have hit the right tone because Aaron clenched and unclenched his fists but finally looked away. "Sandy will be in the parking lot waiting for me."

Mark stole a glance at the clock. He should make Aaron ride to the game with him, but he still needed to shower and shave and that would make the boy late. Aaron didn't need trouble with his coach as well as trouble at home.

"Have Sandy bring you straight home from the game."

"Yeah. Sure." Aaron grabbed his equipment bag and sprinted for the door.

Mark watched Aaron's friend squeal tires as they pulled out of the parking lot. The kid needed new friends.

He'd never realized how hard it was to raise kids until Aaron had moved in a few months ago. Where Mark was usually harsh in his judgment of his sister, and their mother before her, he had to cut her some slack. He could now see how doing the right thing, day in and day out, could wear a person down.

He should at least have made Aaron ride home with him, but now his whole weekend would include a recalcitrant teen in tow. He needed this one night for himself.

Libido. With his family issues, giving in to his libido was

all the indulgence he could give himself where Eva was concerned.

Of course, he had to convince her of the merits of indulging, too.

She felt this attraction between them, too, right? By the way she jumped every time they touched, he was sure of it.

The memory of her mouth on his gave him a boost stronger than a jolt to the heart with the paddles. She had to think of that kiss as often as he did—which was several times a day. Sometimes several times a minute when he needed the lift.

Save two. Who was Eva bringing? Surely not a male friend?

Eva didn't have a kid, did she?

Once upon a time he'd wanted to start a family with Tiffany, but it took two and she hadn't wanted to stall the momentum of her career. So much for happily ever after.

Had Eva's marriage been happy?

He was realizing he knew little about her, only what her public relations profile wanted the general public to know. Except for that night at the pizza parlor, she rarely talked about herself and only as it related to her job.

She might have a house full of little ones and a live-in nanny for all he knew.

He'd never dated a woman with a child. It had seemed too complex and would have taken too much effort.

But Eva was worth a lot of effort.

Besides, Mark didn't mind kids in general, although he wasn't too keen on teen boys right now.

Aaron's supersized tennis shoes lay in the hall where he'd kicked them off.

As he nudged them towards Aaron's room with his toe he realized he *had* a kid now, didn't he?

He cranked up the shower, blasting hot water to work the

kinks out of his neck. Aaron had him more tense than a full moon on Halloween in the E.R.

Thinking of the women he'd taken out, he'd known after their initial dinner and a movie that he would be wasting both their time taking it any further.

But Eva was different.

So different that satisfying his libido wouldn't be enough?

It had to be enough. That's all he had to give.

He finished off his shower by turning the hot water down until the water flowed icy cold over him. After not enough sleep, he could use the burst of energy the freezing water gave him.

As he looked into the mirror to shave, he couldn't ignore the shadows under his eyes.

What was it Eva had told her producer earlier? "He earned them"?

She understood. He'd never had that in a woman—in anyone, actually. He tended to make friends outside work, so the dentist and the accountant and the landscaper he hung with didn't get it. Death didn't stare them in the face every day.

But Eva…

How did she get it? Did her empathy for her late husband's work go so deeply that she had felt what he'd felt? If she had worked in the medical trauma field, she would have said so, wouldn't she? Why did she seem incredibly reluctant to talk about her past career?

While Aaron worked on his paper tomorrow, Mark decided he would do a little internet research, too. A quick search should give him more info on Eva. Or he could just ask her.

Probably the better option.

But talking would mean sharing. Was he really ready for that kind of give and take?

He surprised himself when his answer was a *definite maybe*.

CHAPTER SEVEN

EVA LOOKED AT the moon overhead. The air was just cool and breezy enough to keep the mosquitoes away, which made the night perfect for football.

And for kissing under the bleachers. What sweet memories!

But she wasn't even going to get to indulge in handholding tonight.

"Do you mind sitting on the sidelines?" Mark had asked when he'd met Eva and her niece Selma at the entrance gate and led them to seats on the field.

"Perfect," she'd graciously answered.

And that's the last she'd heard from him.

First, he'd left them to wrap an ankle sprain, then he'd been asked to check out a bruised rib. And then he'd had the inevitable concussion checks to perform after the players' hard tackles.

A seat on the sidelines put Eva and Selma in the center of the action, definitely the best seats in the house. Not only were they the best seats in the house for watching the game but also for observing the cheerleaders up close.

Eva's niece watched the cheer squad, entranced with their dance sequences, their uniforms, and their precision drills. To become a cheerleader was her biggest goal and her Aunt Eva was determined to help.

Good goals and good choices were important to have. Short term, long term, any term. The focus and discipline and, best of all, the pride in achieving that goal shaped psyches, which, in turn, shaped lives.

At her niece's inner-city grade school, the same one Eva had attended, it was too easy to make bad choices.

Bad choices shaped lives just as strongly and the results from accomplishing those bad goals were very hard to recover from.

But there was always hope. Her brother with his thriving little family was proof of that.

Chuck had played a big part in turning her brother away from the street gangs and towards thinking for himself.

As the band took the field for the half-time show, Eva watched Mark follow the team into the locker room.

Nothing like attending a football game with a guy who didn't have time for her. The upside was that her niece got one hundred percent of her attention.

Questions that all began with, "When you were a cheerleader, Aunt Eva, did you...?" kept her busy.

Most of the time the answer was no. They hadn't had three different sets of pompoms. Their pep squad's noisemakers had been made from dried beans stuffed into empty cola cans. They'd only had two sets of uniforms and most of them had been hand-me-downs from the graduating seniors.

Obviously, this first-tier school had a more prosperous booster club than her third-tier high school had had.

But the enthusiasm and heart for the game was the same for the players no matter what school claimed their pride. And a victorious whoop to celebrate a touchdown was the same no matter what part of town a person came from.

Mark took a long look back over his shoulder as he headed to the locker rooms. Wrapped tightly in her long red sweater, Eva looked luscious. He wanted to hold her close, whisper in her ear, make sweet promises to warm her up, to make her hot.

He almost turned to sprint back to her side. But then one of the television station's crew jogged up beside him and asked if he was ready to make his short statement about the signs of concussion.

He'd forgotten. Last Monday, they had asked him to be prepared for this and now he'd have to wing it.

He could use Eva's quick thinking and easy banter for this one.

Mark stopped that line of thinking in its tracks.

It had been a long time since he'd relied on a woman—on anyone—for help. This was his responsibility. He was more than capable of doing this by himself.

"Concussion is taken very seriously in high-school sports. This is one of the primary injuries that could take an athlete out of the game. Long-lasting damage could occur with re-injury. So no matter how key the player might be to our game, no matter how much we want the win, we have to remember that no high-school game, even a championship game, is worth a lifetime of disability."

Even as he said the words he remembered taking risks he shouldn't have during his football years.

"These teen athletes will probably not have the maturity to make such long-range decisions, especially if they are suffering from a brain injury. Parents have a responsibility to make the hard decisions and keep their athletes out of play, even if that's for the remainder of the season."

Mark remembered one hit he'd taken where his ears had rung for days.

His coach had tried to talk to his mother about taking him to the doctor but she had taken little interest in his athletics so she had succumbed to Mark's pleas to let it go just to get him out of the house.

The coach had then demanded Mark's father's phone number and had called him at his private practice to explain and get his support in having Mark X-rayed.

His dad had been furious that his mother hadn't been taking care of the situation. He had been doing his job by sending plenty of money for child support. She should have been doing hers by taking care of things like this.

Mark had heard the whole conversation since his mom had conducted it on conference call mode.

But Mark hadn't wanted to go to the doctor, too afraid of what the tests might show.

He'd said a few strong words of protest—although nothing as bad as the way Aaron generally spoke to his mother—and his dad had agreed to "examine" him over the phone.

So his dad had asked questions. Dizziness? Fainting? Sensitivity to light? Being the tough guy he'd thought he was, seventeen-year-old Mark had told his dad that a couple of aspirin had taken care of any lasting effects and he was fine. Then he'd had to listen to a lecture from both his parents about letting other people meddle in family business.

In the end, the coach had benched him. It had cost him the state record for passes thrown. At the time Mark had been furious. He'd had to do a lot of growing up to understand his coach had made the right decision.

That reminded him. He'd left a note for the school counselor to call him about Sharona, the cheerleader Eva was worried about. How would her parents react to someone getting into *their* business, telling them they didn't know their own daughter well enough to take care of her properly? But what choice did he have when they had refused to return his calls?

Eva wrapped her sweater tighter around her against the nighttime chill as the band marched onto the field for the halftime show. The energetic cheerleaders weren't feeling the cold, though, despite their skimpy uniforms—all except for Sharona.

While the team set up for their pyramid, the girl surreptitiously rubbed her arms as she jumped up and down as she had done at practice. Too thin. Eva's gut instinct continued to shout anorexia. She'd held back as long as she could. Practicing physician or not, she was still a doctor. She had a moral obligation.

As soon as Eva saw Mark, she would ask if he'd talked to the girl's mother yet. If he hadn't, she would.

Interfering in a family's life, uninvited, was always a difficult thing to do, but her years as a substance-abuse doctor had taught her that avoiding problems didn't make them go away.

She sat up straighter. It felt good to think of herself as an experienced doctor. Maybe, someday, she could go back.

The cheerleaders showed off their prowess, making a two-high pyramid like they'd practiced the other day in the gym. With grace and skill the flyer took her pose on top to the wild applause of the crowd.

The team would be coming back to the field welcomed with plenty of school spirit from the crowd.

"One, two, three," the head cheerleader counted, and the flyer dismounted in perfect form while the fans yelled and cheered.

But Sharona made a little wobble then sank to the ground.

Eva was up and racing towards her before she even realized it. "Stay put," she told her niece over her shoulder.

From somewhere behind her she heard a fan yell to one of the girls, "Go get Dr. Mark."

Sharona's skin was pale and cold with the tell-tale sprinkling of fine hair signifying undernourishment.

As Eva was checking for pulse and pupils, the girl regained consciousness.

"Cold," she whispered through blue lips.

Eva whipped off her sweater and wrapped it around the girl and scooped her up to hold her tight. The girl was way too light to pick up for her height and age.

"When did you eat last?"

The girl's eyes went wide. "I'm sure it was just before the game."

One of the girls behind her shook her head. "No, you didn't, Sharona. We all did, but you said you'd already eaten and weren't hungry."

"Someone get me a sports drink," Eva ordered.

Within seconds a plastic bottle was shoved into her hands. She twisted off the cap. "Drink, sweetie."

The girl took a sip. "That's enough."

"One more."

The girl stared off into the night. "One hundred and twenty calories a serving. Two and a half servings in that bottle. I just swallowed at least sixty calories."

Mark arrived at the same time as the girl's parents.

The parents crouched over the girl, who was struggling to get up. Eva put her hand on the girl's bony shoulder. "Sit still until you finish that drink."

"I don't want it." The girl tried to pour it on the ground, but Eva grabbed it from her first.

"What happened?" Mark asked, squatting down next to Eva and the girl.

"We're holding up the game." The father scooped the child up and carried her to the sidelines. Mark and Eva followed him.

"She fainted." Eva addressed the parents, who looked at Mark for answers. "I don't think she's eaten today."

The father turned red in the face. "Of course she's eaten. What do you think we do? Starve our children?"

The girl's mother bit her lip. "She hasn't been eating much lately. She says her jeans are getting too tight."

"As you can see, the issue has gotten out of hand." Eva fished into her purse and found a card for the clinic. "Tell the receptionist Dr. Veracruz recommended you."

"I don't want to see a doctor," Sharona insisted.

"I know you're a bit anxious about all this, but someone at the clinic will talk to you about it."

Eva worked to keep her comments vague yet reassuring. Delivering a diagnosis in the middle of a football game wouldn't be very helpful for the girl. A proper evaluation was needed then long-term therapy if Eva's gut feeling was correct.

The man took the card, read it, then handed it back. "We don't need a free clinic, especially one specializing in drug abuse. Does our daughter look like a druggy?"

Eva looked at the child who desperately needed help. "The clinic has staff that also specialize in eating disorders and other types of self-abuse teens might suffer from."

With an embarrassed shrug the mother told Eva, "You know young girls. They get caught up in the fun and forget to eat. Or it could be her time of the month. That often makes girls light-headed."

With the lack of body fat the girl carried, Eva doubted the teen even had menses.

Mark knelt next to Sharona, cajoling her into drinking a few healthy swallows of the sports drink. Eva totally understood the hero-worship in the girl's eyes.

Eva knew how hard it was for family to recognize a problem that had undoubtedly crept up on them, but she had to get Sharona help. "Maybe I should call an ambulance. It's obvious she needs help."

She whipped out her cellphone, determined to make good on her promise.

The father turned to Mark, "What do you think, Dr. O'Connell?"

Mark gave Eva a look she couldn't interpret before he said, "I don't think we need emergency services here. But I do think you need to have her checked out. Any time some-one faints, a thorough exam is a good idea."

Mark's answer wasn't the most supportive she'd ever heard, but the parents seemed to take him more seriously than her.

Finally, the mother said, "We have our own doctor. I'll make an appointment tomorrow. Please, we need to stop drawing attention to ourselves."

Shakily, Sharona stood and headed back towards her cheer team.

"Wait." Eva reached out to the girl's mother. "She needs to go home, have a good meal and rest."

"But she says she's fine. Her team needs her or they can't do their routines."

Eva propped her hands on her hips, barely holding her temper in check. "They can get along without her for the rest of the game."

Mark reached out to touch the mother's shoulder. "If she faints again, imagine the embarrassment."

That was the prompt that turned the tide. "You're right, Dr. O'Donnell. She might be coming down with something. I hear flu is going around."

As they walked away, Eva said to Mark, "What she's com-ing down with is starvation."

Mark flipped over Eva's card, which the father had handed back to him. "I didn't know you specialized in substance abuse diagnosis and treatment."

"I know. You think I only play a doctor on television."

The futility of trying to help a family who wouldn't ac-knowledge they needed it drew her down. "But, then, that was in a different lifetime."

Mark thumped the card. "Do you think they really need this kind of help?"

"When conditions like anorexia or drug abuse or mental illness happen to teens, they happen to the whole family. A visit to the girl's family doctor for a check-up won't be enough. That girl's hope is that her family doctor has enough influence to convince her parents to take her to a specialist."

She gave her niece a little wave, appreciating that Selma had sat quietly throughout the whole drama. Family counseling worked. Her family was proof of that.

Mark frowned. "We do plenty of referrals in the E.R., usually to the patient's regular doctor, but I don't know how many people follow up."

"Not enough." She patted him on the arm. "I'll get you a handful of cards to distribute when you see a need."

Mark rubbed his thumb along the edge of the card he held. "Got any for a more local clinic? The folks who come to my E.R. aren't likely to drive to this side of town for treatment."

"You'd be surprised." Eva had treated more than one wealthy family, too ashamed of their perceived weaknesses to want anyone in their circle to know. "Our clinic's street address has nothing to do with quality of treatment."

Mark looked chagrined. "That's not what I meant. I'm trying to be realistic. The kids who go to this school, the people who live in this neighborhood are not going to drive into this part of town for treatment. And the important thing is getting treatment, right? So giving them a resource they're unlikely to use wouldn't do them any good, would it?"

Eva had to concede that point.

"Hey, Doc?"

Eva turned toward the sound of the football player's voice, even as she realized the boy was calling for Mark and not for her.

"What's up?"

The player pointed to the field where Aaron had just bulldozed over a player on the other team. The boy lay flattened, unmoving.

"I'm on it."

Mark hustled off to check on the boy while Eva resisted the temptation to follow him. One doctor per patient was sufficient for diagnosis—as long as it was the right doctor. And Mark was the right doctor for checking out sports injuries.

"Aunt Eva, why did that girl faint?"

Eva looked at her beautiful niece. "Because she hasn't been eating right."

"Doesn't she have food? We have enough. Daddy got paid yesterday and Momma went to the grocery store. We could bring her some."

"She has enough food, sweetie." Honesty was the best policy. Her niece would soon be worried about her own changing body. Now was a good time for this discussion. "She's worried about gaining weight as she becomes a woman."

Her niece looked down at her own slightly plump thighs and pudgy child's stomach. She would have a growth spurt during the winter if her growing pattern matched her own and her brother's.

Selma bit the corner of her cheek. "That cheerleader has pretty blonde hair but she doesn't have any boobies. She's not growing up yet."

Eva cocked an eyebrow at her niece. "And getting boobies is what happens as we grow up. We start to look like women. Can't stay little girls all our lives, can we?"

Selma wiggled her shoulders, probably feeling the straps of her training bra. "I want boobies. Boys like them. Momma says you have to eat right to get them."

"Momma's right, but you want to know a secret about boys?"

Selma leaned in as if Eva was going to give her the

golden key to understanding relationships between the sexes. "Tell me."

"Boys like to look at girls' boobies, but that doesn't mean they like the girl inside. If a boy really likes the girl inside, he thinks she looks pretty on the outside, no matter what she really looks like."

"Like Momma and Daddy? He's always calling her his hot tamale."

Eva thought of her sister-in-law, a woman who had given birth to three children, gaining fifteen extra pounds each time. "Like your momma and daddy."

What did Mark like in a woman? Boobs? She hoped so. She had plenty of that. But, then, she needed to believe her own advice.

And there it was. She and Mark had plenty of physical chemistry but was there anything else?

She really knew very little about him and every time he opened his mouth it was obvious he knew nothing about her.

Libido was a terrible thing to have when it had nowhere to go.

CHAPTER EIGHT

THE NEXT TIME Eva saw Mark, the game was over and he was offering to walk her to the parking lot.

"Sure. Why not?" Her response might not be the most gracious in the world but, then, she wasn't feeling very gracious. If her body would follow suit with her attitude, she could have said no instead.

Was it him or was it her?

Maybe she just missed male company and any man would do. But she immediately nixed that idea. She'd had plenty of opportunity for male companionship. This male was the only one who held her interest.

A walk to the parking lot. She was a cheap date—a confused cheap date.

Apparently, this was not a date, as she had assumed.

Just what did constitute a date with him? The pizza thing hadn't been a date and they had kissed. The football game had been a date—she had thought—and they hadn't even held hands.

She was going backwards in exploring any kind of connection. Expectations were getting crossed. Words weren't getting said.

And there was the problem—lack of communication.

For two people whose function was to communicate to the public, neither of them was doing very well with each other.

"I'm over there." She pointed to her car. Sitting next to the new luxury sedan, it looked tiny and vulnerable.

And it had a flat tire.

"Give me your keys and I'll change it for your spare."

The gesture was gallant, but— "That is the spare."

She looked down at a worried Selma. "Gotta call your daddy."

With great pride Selma explained to Mark. "Daddy can fix anything."

Much better than Daddy needs a fix. Her brother had been clean for almost ten years, ever since before his daughter was even born. Eva felt pride for all he had accomplished.

She hit speed dial on her phone. "Hey, bro. You know that tire you were going to replace for me as soon as I found the time to drive by your shop? Well, I should have made time sooner."

She gave directions to the high-school football field.

Turning to Mark, she told him, "Ricky's on wrecker duty tonight and not too far away. He'll be here in ten minutes. You don't have to wait with us."

"Sure I do. I would never leave a woman stranded."

Was it her or was she getting mixed signals?

Was that what she was to him? A generic woman?

How badly did she want to change that?

Pretty badly. Put it down to ego, but she wanted to be more than that to Mark.

Selma started twitching. "I don't like this. It feels creepy."

Parking lots in her neighborhood *were* creepy. But this one was safe enough even if the security light near Eva's car was out.

Mark gave Selma a reassuring smile as he pointed up. "Want to know what that constellation is called?"

"Okay." She craned her neck to see where he was pointing.

He lifted her up so she could lie back on the hood of Eva's

car. "See the ones in a row? All those stars together are called Orion's Belt."

Eva looked up where he pointed. As she did so, she felt his hand slip to her waist and pull her close.

Maybe she should resist, but the warmth of his palm felt too good, too masculine to step away from.

It was nice to not feel lonely.

Again, he pointed to the night sky, which jostled Eva even closer to him. "And that really bright star is not a star at all. It's a planet. If you stay really still, you can see it move. Stars don't appear to move, only planets."

With mixed feelings Mark recognized the rattle of a wrecker as it pulled into the parking lot. While he was just about to run out of his limited knowledge of stars, he wasn't even close to running out of the desire to hold Eva close to him.

"He's here." Selma sat up on the car hood and waved in the truck's direction.

The driver waved back.

As Eva's brother climbed out, Mark couldn't help but notice the tattoos crawling down both arms. They were crude, like prison tattoos.

"My rescuer." Eva threw her arms around the man's neck.

Mark shifted on his feet.

Rescuer. That was usually his role.

"I got here as quick as I could." The man gave Mark a strong stare.

Mark gave it back.

Eva gave them both a worried look. "Mark, meet my brother, Ricky."

She put her hand on her brother's arm. "I told you about Mark, remember? He's doing the television spot with me."

"Oh, that Mark. Your co-worker." Ricky held out his hand to shake. "Nice to meet you."

Mark took Ricky's callused hand. "You, too."

Co-worker.

Mark wanted it to be more. He just wasn't sure how much more.

Ricky squatted down to look at the tire.

Mark pointed to the nail protruding through the side wall. "I'm pretty sure that's the problem."

Ricky looked up at him with a masculine version of Eva's smile. "Ya think?"

Mark had to laugh. Was the whole family as smart-mouthed as Eva was? "I guess that was a little obvious."

Ricky shook his head. "I'll have to round up a tire and rim in the morning. Should have done it last week."

Eva patted him on the shoulder. "It was a bad week. Just take me home when you drop off Selma and I'll catch a taxi to work in the morning."

Mark stepped forward. "I'll take you home."

Eva stayed silent a beat too long as she gave him a sexy half-smile. "It's only a ride home?"

Was she asking for more? By her tone, he was sure of it. "Maybe dinner between here and there."

Ricky cleared his throat. "Flirting in front of the k-i-d?"

Eva's eyes sparkled as she playfully punched him on the shoulder. "That k-i-d sees enough flirting at home to be used to it. It's like you and Susan have been married for only a few months instead of ten years."

Ricky didn't look old enough to have been married that long.

He must have guessed Mark's question, because he said without prompting, "Teenagers in love."

Mark didn't know what to say. "It seems to have worked out for you."

Ricky glanced down then over to Eva while rubbing the

letters crudely inked into his knuckles. "Not without a lot of help. Still working on it, day by day."

Eva reached over and hugged him, reinforcing whatever Ricky was overcoming with sisterly strength.

What would it be like to have a family like that?

The last time he'd hugged his sister had been at a cousin's wedding when the photographer had instructed him to stand closer and put his arm around her so they could all squeeze into the shot.

"Pizza?" she asked.

"How about some place where the kids aren't? I know this Greek restaurant that has the best baklava."

She leaned up and whispered in his ear, "Keep sweet-talking me with dessert and you may get to walk me to my door afterward."

"Does that include a goodnight kiss?" *Or a good-morning one?* he wanted to add. He still couldn't get past her introducing him to Ricky as her co-worker. Maybe Eva was right to play down this thing between them.

Eva sent him a look over her shoulder as she headed toward her car to gather her things.

Then again, they only had a few more weeks of working together. Besides, the problems arose when the couple had nothing more than work to tie them together. He and Eva had more than work between them. They had chemistry with a capital C.

All doctors knew the importance of good chemistry, right?

And they all knew what happened when chemistry went bad, too.

Mark realized he was finally starting to think about his ex-wife simply as someone that he used to know.

It seemed the laws of chemistry held true. Things did finally stop exploding when the fire went out.

Before Eva made it back to him, Ricky sidled close. "Take care of my sister or I'll take care of you. Got it?"

Mark remembered saying the same thing to all his sister's dates. Being the man of the house, it had been his job to ensure the safety of her and his mother. Although, with the men they picked, it had been damned hard.

So instead of being offended, he appreciated Ricky's warning. "Got it. I've got a sister of my own."

Ricky patted him on the back as if he'd just been admitted to a special club. "Three daughters, in addition to my sister and grandmother. The women in our families—they're a handful, but they're worth it, aren't they?"

Mark gave a noncommittal grunt as he thought of his own mother, who had clearly not wanted his opinion on her newest husband, and of his sister and the son she had turned over to him.

What would it be like to have a daughter, one with Eva's laughing eyes?

He shook off the thought. He hadn't even begun their first official date yet.

Although she was tall enough not to need it, Eva accepted Mark's hand to help her into his truck.

His hand, large, warm and very strong, made her own hand feel fragile. It took quite a man to make her feel delicate.

His palm on her waist made her want to turn round, chest to chest, pelvis to pelvis.

Instead of indulging, she slid into the truck seat and immediately buckled her seat belt.

Mark cocked an eyebrow.

She grinned at him. "I might need the restraint to keep my hands off you long enough for you to drive us to the restaurant."

Flirting felt so good. So fun. Even after all their years of marriage, she and Chuck had never lost their ability to flirt.

Instead of making her feel sad, like thoughts of Chuck usually did, she felt sweet nostalgia.

Everyone had said recovery would happen. It just took time.

She hadn't believed them.

But Mark was making her a believer.

After driving through the Garden District, Mark turned into a tiny, crowded gravel parking lot on the edge of a residential neighborhood. The small sign said, "Olympia's".

Mark edged his truck into a slot between two cars. "It's always packed, but worth the wait."

"I've got all night." Saturday would include a morning of house cleaning, a visit to her grandmother and then…

Maybe, just maybe, she would take a drive past the clinic. Maybe she would make it by this time without falling to pieces.

She'd thought she had lost it. Lost her desire to practice medicine. Lost her desire for—well, for everything.

But Mark was giving her back her passion.

When he talked of his night's work in the E.R., his zeal for making the world better, one patient at a time, he made her want to do the same.

And when he touched her, the sparks he sent along her skin made her want to do the same, too.

Mark put his arm around her as they zigzagged through the maze of cars.

Dinner. Then what?

Was it the right time? Too soon?

Indecision swamped her.

The only thing she was sure of was that Mark was the right man.

How did she know? Gut feeling. One of those innate comprehensions that defied reasoning. One of those things all doctors learned to trust.

She had lost that trust in herself. Why did she have it back now?

Mark. There was no other answer.

Eva was so easy to talk to. Maybe too easy. Mark found himself telling her things he'd never thought he would talk about.

He gave her an intensely probing stare. "Family is everything to me. It's my backbone. My foundation."

It had been the thing that had broken his marriage.

Eva nodded. "Me, too. My brother and sister-in-law and my nieces are my world. My grandmother, too, although she has dementia and doesn't know any of us any more."

"That's tough."

"Yes, it is. When she forgets me, forgets I exist, in my head I know it's the disease. But in my heart it makes me feel unimportant to her."

Mark had thought that about his father, too, even though his father was hale and hearty. The day he'd married his new wife and moved to Florida had been the day Mark had felt like he'd lost his dad.

"I'm sure deep down, in the place that's buried under the physical, she still knows you. She must be very proud of you."

"She is. While she couldn't financially help with medical school, she gave me the moral support that kept me going. She would come over and wash our clothes. Leave food in the fridge. Let me know she was praying for me." Eva's heart filled with emotion. "She taught me about unconditional love. It's what she's made of."

"She taught you well. It's obvious you return it. And give it to your brother and his family as well."

"There was a time when that unconditional love had to battle it out with tough love. While they're not mutually exclusive, it felt like that at the time." Eva took advantage of this opening to hint about Aaron. "At first we didn't realize Ricky was into drugs. Not that he hid it—he's just not that way. But it happened gradually and, being family, we didn't want to see the worst in him."

"I love my family, but I have to admit we have our faults. We *don't* put the fun in dysfunctional. We're not typical, I guess." Mark gave her sympathy even though he couldn't understand how a person could live with a drug addict and not realize it.

"We had thought we were unique, the only family in the world drug addiction had ever happened to. But we *are* typical. Denial happens in most families. But it only makes coming back from the brink a harder and longer process."

"Did Ricky inspire you to go into the field of substance-abuse treatment?"

She shook her head. "It was my husband, many years before we married. I had just graduated high school and was trying to find a job when I met Chuck. He was a beat cop in my neighborhood, older than me by eight years but I looked older. He looked younger. And in the end age made no difference.

"He saw everyone as humans, individuals, no matter what shape they were in. My best friend in high school, a girl with a brilliant future in front of her, got hooked on meth. Instead of treating her like trash, Chuck treated her like a girl with a problem. He must have had her taken to the hospital at least three dozen times before she finally overdosed and couldn't be saved.

"He held me when I cried. Told me I could make a difference. Taught me about financial aid and scholarships and helped me enroll in college. I had never even considered going to college before that. I didn't know anyone who had."

Even knowing he had no right, Mark felt both gratitude

and jealousy toward this paragon. How could he compete with the memory of a dead man?

"Why did you quit medicine? When you talk about treating families, I can see the passion in your eyes."

The waiter brought their order of baklava to the table, interrupting the moment.

Eva sat back and picked up a piece of baklava. "This isn't really the way I intended this conversation to go."

She took a bite and gave a moan any man would want to wring from her lips.

Mark promised himself he would do everything in his power to bring that kind of ecstasy to her eyes. "Good, huh?"

"Absolutely." She picked up a piece and held it to his lips. "Try it."

If it had been the apple from Eden, Mark wasn't sure he could have resisted.

Her fingertips against his mouth sent a rush through his system, speeding it up, making it pump, making him restless for her.

"Good?"

He wrested his focus back to the rich sweetness in his mouth. "Yes. Absolutely," he said, repeating her word.

The baklava was as good as he remembered it. The dating game was even better than he remembered it.

"Hmm..." Eva licked the stickiness from her lips.

Mark watched, entranced, as the tip of her tongue swept across her lip. It was like the basketball game all over again.

"Good?" he asked, wanting to hear her voice.

"Very." The huskiness in her tone exceeded his expectations.

He hoped to hear it tonight and maybe in the morning, too.

That's when he remembered how much had changed since the last time he'd dated. Then he'd had an apartment all to himself. Now he had a teenager living under his roof. It would have to be Eva's place tonight and morning sex would be out.

Raising this kid really cramped his style.

As if he'd conjured up Aaron with his thoughts, his phone buzzed, showing his nephew's cellphone number.

"Uncle Mark?" Aaron's voice quivered. He sounded young. Scared.

The controlled calm that came over him in emergencies settled into Mark's mind. "Yes, Aaron?"

"Uh, I'm at the police station and they said I could call you."

"You're where?" Mark asked, even though he'd heard it clearly the first time. This was not the type of emergency he was prepared to handle. How had his sister done it that first time she'd received a call like this?

"Dr. O'Donnell, this is Officer Stack. This is a courtesy call. Your nephew was stopped for driving erratically. He is being charged with driving under a suspended license, resisting an officer and violating the terms of his probation. We have your nephew at the Fifth Precinct annex. We are about to book him and send him to a juvenile facility. Would you like to come down and talk to him first?"

"Yes. I'll be right there."

Mark hung up the phone and blinked for a split second, forgetting where he was and who he was with. Now the enormity of the situation came crashing down on him.

"Mark, what's wrong?"

"I've got to go."

"Okay. I guess I can call a taxi."

"No, I'll…" Mark looked up as if the ceiling tiles held all the answers. "Where is the Fifth Precinct annex?"

"In my neighborhood."

Mark was surprised at the address she gave him. The rough part of town. What was Aaron doing there?

Later, he would think about why Eva still lived there. If there was a later for them after this. Most likely she would drop him like a hot stone when she found out about his family troubles. He couldn't blame her. Who wanted to be associated with his kind of problems?

"Is it Aaron?" Eva pushed back her chair and put her purse strap over her shoulder.

Numbly, Mark nodded.

"Let's go, then. I can give you a few shortcuts through the streets."

"Those are not streets I'd want to cut through with you in the truck. That's not the safest part of town."

"That part of town is my home. Where I grew up. Where I live. Where my brother lives." She gave him a twisted smile. "Come on, big boy. I'll protect you."

Her humor fell flat. But she had already taken the lead, heading out of the restaurant in front of him.

Throwing enough bills on the table to cover their meal, he followed her.

He helped her into the truck then drove as if on autopilot towards the precinct.

At one red light a group of teens on bikes crowded the truck. Before he could stop her, Eva rolled down her window.

"Get out of the street before you get hit." She raised her hand against the glare of the streetlight. "Maria Rosita, is that you? Just wait until I tell your father you were out this late."

The kids scattered before the light turned green.

"Maria's father works the night shift. He will ground her for a month when he finds out she was out tonight."

Absently, Mark responded, "You're going to tell him?"

"Of course. Wouldn't you want someone to tell you if your teenager was out so late without permission?"

"You mean, someone other than the police? Yes, I guess I would."

Mark thought of the time the neighbor had called his mother about him climbing out his girlfriend's upstairs window when he was fourteen. She had railed about busybodies for hours and had then had the woman kicked out of the Junior League and had never spoken to her again.

Chances were Maria Rosita's father didn't know anyone in the Junior League. And, yes, now that he was in the parental role, he could see where he might appreciate a warning call even though it would be a very uncomfortable conversation.

Once at the station Mark didn't know what to do with Eva.

It turned out that he didn't need to do anything. As soon as he put the truck into park, she was out and heading for the front doors.

He hurried his stride to catch up with her.

The guard at the door nodded to them both as they went through the security scanner.

"It's been a while, Doc," he said to Eva.

"Yes, it has, Henry."

Even though Mark wanted to know more, now was not the time to stop and ask questions.

The fluorescent lights cast the same harsh light over everything and everyone in the precinct annex as they did in the emergency department.

Clarity. In-your-face reality. No shadows to obscure problems that needed to be addressed.

The atmosphere was familiar to Mark, but the procedures were not. Here, surrounded by professionals in dark uniforms and holstered guns instead of scrubs and stethoscopes, he felt like a victim instead of a rescuer.

His ex-wife stood at the reception desk. She was dressed in some kind of black silky dress that showed off her cleavage and mile-high shoes that showed off her legs.

She had her lawyer face on, the face that would win national poker tournaments if she were to lower herself to participate in such a plebian activity.

She greeted him with, "He's fine."

"Why are you here?" All his worry and frustration came out in his question.

"Aaron called me."

"I can handle this."

"I've known Aaron from the day he was born. We might not be husband and wife any more, but he will always be my nephew despite that piece of paper between you and me. Let me help."

Mark was acutely aware of Eva by his side, witnessing this whole exchange.

The desk clerk stared at him until he gave her his attention. "Sir, I understand you're Aaron Cunningham's legal guardian. Would you like to go back and see your nephew?"

"Yes, please."

Eva watched him go, her heart going with him.

The woman held out her hand. "Tiffany Spears, Mark's ex-wife."

Eva accepted the firm handshake. "Eva Veracruz."

Tiffany nodded. "I've seen you testify in court before. Substance-abuse expert, right?"

Eva nodded. It had been a while since she'd considered herself an expert, though.

Eva could see the change in Tiffany's eyes as she remembered where else she'd seen Eva.

"I'm sorry about your husband."

"Thank you." She looked Tiffany in the eyes. "And it's long overdue, but also thank you for handling the case so well."

"Killers should be taken out of society, especially cop killers." Tiffany glanced at her buzzing phone. "Excuse me, please."

Eva took a seat on one of the hard plastic chairs where she could see Mark when he came back from his visit with Aaron.

Her eyes skimmed over the posters on the walls warning against shoplifting or illegal gun possession or a half-dozen other crimes. She'd sat here plenty of times before, waiting for Chuck to end his shift, waiting to drive him home, knowing he'd had a long heart-breaking day. Waiting to give comfort where she could.

And now she waited on Mark for the same reason.

Tiffany seated herself next to Eva.

"Been dating long?"

Eva tensed, not sure where this was going. "No. We're co-workers." Not feeling truthful about that not-quite-right answer, she followed with, "Tonight's our first real date."

"Mark's a great guy." Tiffany bit her lip, a gesture that looked out of place with her confident persona. "It was completely my fault."

"There's no such thing." Eva gave her a reassuring smile. "I've done enough counseling to know that—and I was married enough years to know that, too."

Tiffany waved away Eva's reasoning. "Mark was and still is all about family. He's the glue that holds his mother and sister together. I wanted to be first in his life. I couldn't share. So I found someone else, except it didn't work out."

"I really don't need to know this."

"The way he looks at you, and the way you look back at him, there's something between the two of you."

"Maybe there will be, but not right now." As Eva said it, it sounded false. The sparks they shared weren't glimmers of the future. They were full-blown electric shocks happening right now.

That's why she could tell, simply from the footfalls in the hallway, that Mark was approaching them.

As soon as he rounded the corner, his face pale and drained, she stood and forced an encouraging smile for him.

Tiffany watched him with guarded eyes, glanced at Eva, then put her phone away.

When Mark spotted Eva, he walked towards her like a man dying of thirst walking toward a dry river bed.

His eyes were bleak, hopeless, but wishing for a miracle.

Without thought, she opened her arms to him and he moved in for her embrace.

As Tiffany walked towards them, he pushed himself away.

"Would he talk to you?" she asked.

"Yes." Mark rubbed his hand through his hair. "He just doesn't get it. He thinks this is no big deal and he's being unfairly persecuted."

Tiffany let out a sigh. "Do you want me to represent him? You have to tell me that officially."

What would have seemed an obvious yes to Eva gave Mark pause. He seemed to be fixated on a poster of a young man being led away in handcuffs for vehicular homicide. It read, "Barely buzzed is still drunk."

"Mark?" Tiffany put her hand towards him then dropped it.

"Yes." He looked at her, his eyes brimming with tears. "Yes, I'll hire you to represent him."

"We'll talk about the hiring part later," she said. "In anticipation, I've made some calls. They'll keep him overnight in juvenile detention and tomorrow you can take him home on your own recognizance."

Mark's eyes hardened. "I want to take him home tonight."

"This is his second offense." Tiffany took a breath. "You won't like to hear this, but Aaron's so hard-headed that a night locked up might be a good lesson in taking responsibility for his actions."

"Tough love, Tiffany? What about family loyalty? That one's not as high on your list, is it?"

Tiffany clenched her mouth tight. "That's the best I can do for Aaron tonight. You can pick him up between ten and ten-thirty tomorrow morning."

Mark paced off to stare out the glass doors into the black night.

Tiffany reached into her purse and handed Eva her card. "I know he's hurting. I'm glad he's got you to take care of him. I wish I could have but it's just not in me."

Eva could tell Tiffany was hurting, too. She tried to reassure her. "We all have our own talents. Mark and Aaron will definitely need yours in the coming days."

"I'll be there for them as much as I can be." Tiffany stared at Mark's back with sad resignation. "Different people fit together differently."

How did she and Mark fit together? Well, so far. But, then, their relationship hadn't been tested.

They hadn't even called what they had between them a relationship.

Tiffany walked toward the doors, putting her hand on Mark's shoulder as she walked past him. "Take care of yourself, Mark. And take good care of Eva, too. She's been through a lot."

Absently, Mark nodded. Taking care of people was what he did. Two patrol officers brushed past him as they entered the building, their faces grim.

He was very ready to get out of this place yet strongly reluctant to leave without his nephew. But he had to take care of Eva. He had to get her out of there.

A yell from the hallway startled them all.

"Help. He's seizing."

Mark took off at a run with Eva right behind them.

Mark's first thought was one of relief. The boy wasn't Aaron.

His next was to help.

But Eva was already on her knees next to the boy, who couldn't have been over sixteen. He lay curled in a fetal position, shaking so hard his body looked blurred.

The boy prised his eyes open, took one look at Mark and the officers surrounding him and seem to shrink even further in on himself.

Mark knelt down on the boy's other side and checked his pupils. "He's responding to light."

"History?"

The officer shook his head sadly. "He lives on the streets. We bring him in a lot, but he's never done this before."

"What do you bring him in for?"

"Usually drunk and disorderly. He begs for money on street corners and the local businesses don't like it."

She smelled his breath. No alcohol. "How long has he been locked up?"

"Since late last night. We're trying to keep him as long as we can so we can get a few meals in him before he's brought before a judge, fined and returned to his father. Then he'll run away and we'll see him back in here within the week sporting new bruises on top of the old ones. Same old cycle over and over with this kid."

"Not seizing. He's got D.T.s." Eva laid her hand on his head, gently brushing his hair off his face. The boy moaned softly, turning his face into her hand like a wounded animal needing reassurance.

"We're going to take care of you," she said softly. "You've called the paramedics, right?" she asked the officer in the same soothing voice.

When he nodded, she asked, "Can we get a couple of blankets?"

The desk office rushed to get the requested blankets.

Eva cushioned the boy's head with one and covered his body with the other.

Feeling helpless, Mark sat back on his heels. There was nothing else to do for the boy. If he were in the E.R. the boy would have already been shipped off to a ward.

But Eva kept patting the boy, rubbing his shoulder, talking quietly, giving him what he needed.

"I'm a doctor," she told him. "And I know how to take care of you. You're going to a detox facility. Have you ever been to one before?"

The boy managed to shake his head despite his trembling.

"They're going to teach you how to get well."

The boy looked up at her with so much hope that Mark felt himself tear up.

"And I'm going to make sure you have someplace safe to go to after you get well."

This time the boy gave her a look of disbelief.

The office standing beside them caught the look. "If Doc Veracruz says it, kid, she means it."

The boy gave her the slightest of smiles.

Then the paramedics came in, all hustle and bustle.

Eva frowned them into silence. "Gently, guys. He's having a bad night."

Under her watchful eye, the paramedics put the boy on the gurney.

Mark turned to her. "I'll take you home now."

"Just one moment, okay?"

Eva walked towards the front desk.

The officer turned to Mark. "That's quite a woman there. She's got the rep of being the best substance-abuse doctor in the area. Works mostly with juveniles. Never gives up on them. It's a real shame she's not practicing any more. But who can blame her, huh?"

Thankfully, the man didn't seem to expect an answer because Mark had none for him.

He knew so little about her. Then, again, he knew so much.

He knew what she was made of. Compassion and strength and brilliance.

And passion in everything she did.

She talked to the woman and the two officers who had just entered, giving them pleading smiles and gesturing with her hands. By the time she'd finished talking, they were nodding with her, agreeing to whatever she'd asked.

Both men gave her strong hugs and the desk clerk patted her hand.

She met him at the door. "I'm ready now."

Mark wanted to ask, but he wasn't sure he could take in any more information at the moment. He felt exhausted, over-extended, off balance. Even his worst night in the E.R. wasn't as bad as this night.

"I don't live far from here."

Eva gave him simple directions and they ended up in front of a set of brick apartment buildings. Flower baskets hung from the stair rails, brightening up the plain exterior.

Mark parked and got out to open the door for her.

Instead of taking his hand to climb out of his truck, she said, "Come up with me for a moment."

"I don't think tonight's the night for that."

"I've got some experience in what will happen next with Aaron. We can talk."

Mark thought about the days ahead. They would not be easy. The more he knew, the better. "Okay."

When Eva took his hand, it seemed more like she was helping him onto solid ground than he was helping her out of his truck.

Help. Not something he was good at accepting.

But he guessed that was about to change.

CHAPTER NINE

EVA'S APARTMENT WAS on the cluttered side. Magazines and mail on the kitchen table. Tennis shoes in the living room. A blanket and pillow on the couch.

Mark had slept on his couch plenty after the divorce. While he would have told his buddies, if they had asked, that he'd fallen asleep watching television, the truth was the bed had seemed too big and cold.

Eva laid her sweater across the top of a recliner in the living room. "It's a little late for coffee. How about decaf tea?"

"Sure." Tea, particularly decaf, wasn't his thing, but it would give him something to do with his hands. He usually wasn't the fidgety sort, but he usually didn't have nights like tonight either.

Eva filled a kettle with water and put it on the stove top. "Have a seat anywhere."

Mark moved a romance novel off the couch, deciding he liked the lived-in look. He'd grown up in a house that had looked like a photograph in a designer magazine. His mom's interior designer had put the rooms together for an outsider's admiration instead of for the family's comfort.

No designer had ever come within a hundred yards of Eva's house. Her style was what his mother would sneeringly call garage-sale chic. But Eva called it home—a much better style, in his opinion.

He leaned back, stretching his legs out in front of him. Eva's house gave him a vibe like he was welcome to stop in any time, no need to call ahead.

The kettle began to sing so Eva poured the hot water into two oversized give-away mugs and then floated the tea bags on top.

She handed him a mug before seating herself at the other end of the couch. "I always thought the best part of hot tea was the dunking part. Otherwise I prefer it iced with lots of sugar."

Obligingly, he dunked the tea bag. "You've got experience in police matters?"

"And in teens in trouble."

"Aaron's not..." Mark swallowed. "I guess he is, isn't he?"

Eva explored the contents of her mug as she dunked her tea bag. "Ricky spent three years in prison for drug distribution." She looked up from her mug. "My husband was the one to arrest him and take him in."

Mark sipped at his overly strong tea. "And I thought I was having a bad day."

"We'd been married about three months by then. I was in my first year of residency, working at the free clinic. Ricky had just turned eighteen and his girlfriend—now his wife, Susan—was four months pregnant with Selma. It was a wild ride." She set her mug on the floor rug. "It wasn't Ricky's first offense but it was his last. Getting him off the streets saved his life."

Mark mulled over what she'd said, trying to see how that related to Aaron. "But Aaron doesn't do drugs."

"Have you had him tested?"

"I'd know. I'm a doctor, trained to see that kind of thing."

"There's a reason doctors frown on treating anyone close

to them. Objectivity and family don't mix." She clasped her hands together. "Aaron might not do drugs, but he does trouble. And that will land him in places he shouldn't be in. And it might get him injured or even killed."

"You're being a bit dramatic here, aren't you? All he was doing was driving too fast. Then he got mouthy, like a lot of teens do." Mark gripped his mug. His own mouth was saying things he'd rather it didn't but he couldn't seem to stop himself. "I'm not the one who needs the lecture."

"A lecture won't do it. In general, teenagers don't listen. He needs some heavy-duty counseling. The whole family needs it. And he needs to be evaluated for drugs of all kinds, illegal and over-the-counter. Not just the standard drug test."

"He's not doing drugs. He wouldn't even know where to get them. He's just a kid." Mark rubbed the tension that was drawing his eyebrows together. He felt anger rise in him, an anger that had no clear direction. "He had some bruises. They may have roughed him up a little."

"I know the men who brought him in. They only did what they had to." Eva reached for Mark's hand, but he kept it tightly gripped around his mug. "He's six-two and over two hundred twenty pounds. And he was out of control. What if one of those policemen had needed to use force to contain him tonight? What if he'd resisted worse than he did? A situation like that can escalate out of control in a heartbeat."

Mark would need names to give to Tiffany for a follow-up investigation. "How do you know those officers?"

"They worked with my husband."

"What did you tell them as we were leaving?"

"To keep him safe tonight. Private cell. Twenty-four-hour monitoring. As a special favor to me."

"They'd do that for you?"

"I'm a policeman's widow as well as a respected doctor. They'd do a lot for me."

"But not release him to me tonight."

"I didn't ask for that."

"Why not?"

"Because I want to do what's best for Aaron and I don't think getting off with nothing but a ride to the police station would be enough for him."

"Tough love? Like your brother in prison? You don't even know him. Aaron's not like that."

"Not like what? Disrespectful of authority? Not interested in school? Thinking he's smarter than the average cop on the street? Wanting the thrill of going outside the boundaries of the law? Putting himself and others in danger?"

Mark gripped the mug so tightly that finer china would have crushed. Yes, Aaron *was* like that.

He had the strongest urge to put his arm around Eva and pull her close, to feel her strength, to find comfort there.

He settled for laying his arm along the back of the couch.

Eva crossed her leg under her, which inched her towards him.

"So what's going to happen next?"

"Your wife—"

"Ex-wife."

"Your ex-wife is talking to the right people to have Aaron released to you. If the judge agrees to release Aaron into your custody, you'll be responsible for enforcing whatever restrictions they give him. That could be anything from a curfew to house arrest."

"House arrest."

"It's up to the judge, who will probably consider recommendations of the attorneys. Odds are the judge will agree to release Aaron to you. Jails are crowded and first-timers can pick up too many bad habits from repeat offenders." She rubbed between her eyes. "But, then, he's not a first-time offender, is he? I don't know what the judge will do. It's according to who you get."

"You had him put by himself. There's a danger that if he's put with those repeat offenders, possibly gang members, they could hurt him?"

Reluctantly, Eva nodded. "It's a possibility."

Mark took a sip of tea but had a hard time swallowing it. "If the judge lets him out, then what happens?"

"You'll get a court date. In the meantime, your lawyer will be talking to the juvenile district attorney's office, trying to sort things out before court."

"What are some of the typical deals?"

"Counseling is a big one and goes with almost every deal. Family as well as individual and group therapy. Community service happens fairly often."

"What kind of community service?"

"Various things. Working at the animal shelter. Painting the recreation centers around town. Working in a food kitchen on weekends. It's really up to the judge and their creativity."

"Aaron could use some of that."

"Mark, I don't want to oversimplify this. Assaulting a police officer is serious. Jail time is possible."

"How will he go to school?"

"They have alternative schools inside the facilities. They've got to reach the maximum amount of students with their curriculum and a lot of these kids haven't spent too much time inside a classroom, so the education isn't the standard Aaron is used to."

"If that happens, he won't be able to play football."

"There *is* more to life than high-school football."

"Not to Aaron. It's the only threat that's worked to keep

him in line. Ever since he was small, when my sister or I needed him to co-operate, we bribed him with the promise of private coaching time." Mark felt like a total failure. "Maybe it's time for a different method than threats and bribes."

"Actually, a reward/punishment system is not a bad way to parent." She scooted over next to him, resting her head on his shoulder.

"My sister is on a cruise. That's why I haven't even bothered to call her. What could she do?"

"Fly home?"

"To do what? Wring her hands and give me another person to take care of?"

He drew in a breath, drawing in the scent of her shampoo, drawing in the logic and order he needed to calm the chaos of his racing thoughts.

Eva gave him a probing look. What was she searching for?

Then she blinked and Mark saw sympathy there. He didn't want her sympathy.

She leaned in close, inviting a comforting kiss.

What he wanted was her body. Her mouth. Her breath mingling with his. All those were a definite yes. But he wasn't into sympathy sex.

Instead of meeting her lips with his own, he looked away.

His throat ached in protest.

She put her hand on his, probably unaware she'd even made contact.

He didn't move his away. He may not take sympathy kisses, but he soaked up her sympathetic touch, especially when it came with that undertone of energy that poured life into his much-bruised spirit.

Mark found himself explaining, "We're not much into sharing the load in my family, only into assigning blame."

Why did he tell her these things? And why did he feel

okay, even better, once he had, as if in the telling, he was lightening his load?

"Believe me, therapy can help with that. When everyone gets their say in a safe environment, a lot of that lopsidedness will begin to even out."

"Tell me about family therapy." Mark couldn't even envision talking about his feelings in front of a stranger and letting that person judge the dynamics of their relationships.

"It's different for everyone. The therapist may try to draw out thoughts and opinions each family member has kept private from each other to work out any underlying resentment or to make sure everyone's needs are met. He or she may give practical tips for making things work better for everyone. Mandatory drug tests for Aaron. Maybe individual counseling for you and Aaron's mother, too. It varies."

"You've done it?"

She nodded. "Been the therapist and the patient."

"You were the patient when your brother got into trouble?"

"And when my husband died."

"How did it happen?"

"How did what happen?" she asked, her mind slow to click over from Aaron to herself.

But she made the switch before Mark clarified, "How did your husband die?"

Eva recognized Mark's change of direction for what it was—self-preservation. The human psyche could only take so much intensity before it had to pull back.

"That's a discussion for a different day." Someday she would be able to talk about it. How many times would she tell herself about the someday that never seemed to come along before she stopped believing herself?

Or had it already happened? Indecision was one of the

most crippling symptoms of PTSD, right up there with the nightmares and the flashbacks. Would Mark understand?

Somehow, she thought he might. What made her think that?

Gut instinct. While PTSD may have crippled her in many ways, she still had her gut instinct. She just had to be brave enough to trust it.

"You're not over it yet, then," Mark said.

Her instincts told her Mark needed some deep-down honesty to be with her. But her hesitation was pushing him away.

Mark shrugged his shoulders and rubbed at his neck. "I guess I'd better get home. I'm not sure why, though. This kind of thing makes an empty house even emptier, doesn't it?"

Could she do it? Could she go with her impulse?

Eyes half-closed, she murmured to him, "If you leave, my house will be empty, too."

Indecision flickered across his eyes. "Are you asking me to stay?"

She pulled her answer up from the core. "My husband gave me what I needed back then. But I'm not the same woman he married. I need something different. I need *someone* different." Eva expected to feel guilty about admitting that. Instead, she felt more like the self she wanted to be.

"Yes. Stay." She laced her fingers through his. "Please."

"Why?" Even though he hadn't moved at all, Eva felt like he was on the verge of pulling away.

"Why?" Did she need to spell it out? She swallowed down her sudden shyness. "Because I want you to touch me in all the right places. And I want to touch you back. I want to fill those empty places in you. And I want you to fill my empty places, too."

As she looked into his eyes, they darkened so much she

thought she might be falling into infinity. His voice was low and slow as he answered, "I'd like that."

She gulped as a moment of panic overcame her. This was really going to happen. Did she really want this?

Then the panic turned into excitement as she thought about Mark's hands on her body, cupping her breasts, running down the length of her thighs.

Yes, this was really going to happen and she wanted it. Now. With this man, who fit her like yin and yang. She wanted it, wanted it so badly it made her ache for his touch, his taste, his feel inside her.

Shivers started way down low, curling deep inside her. "I don't believe I've shown you my bed yet. King-sized with a very firm mattress."

She pulled him up off the couch. Not releasing his hand, she led him into her bedroom.

Her unmade bed looked ready, like it had been waiting for them.

She shoved her sleep shirt off the bed onto the floor then turned to him. "Not the sexiest of nighties, is it?"

"You're the hostess here. You set the dress standards."

"In that case, you're overdressed."

He whipped his shirt off. "Better?"

"Yes. Much. House rules and all."

"I've got good company manners that way." He gave her a grin that had a very serious undertone. "May I help you with your own shirt?"

"Yes, please. That would be lovely." Mark's knuckles grazed her stomach as he caught the edge of her T-shirt and pulled it up.

Obligingly, she raised her arms as he freed her from the restriction.

Mark's face become passionate, entranced. "Wow."

He reached out a finger to trace the cup of her bra. She leaned forward, wanting, wanting.

But he stopped millimeters short. "May I?"

"Yes, please." She let a groan escape. "Oh, yes, please."

"Like this?" Mark's voice had a thin veneer of teasing that didn't cover up the strain of restraint.

He swept his finger along the lacy cups, letting his palms graze her nipples.

His touch left her aching, needing— "More."

"More? Like this?" He leaned in and kissed her, starting with her neck right below her ear then trailing kisses down her cleavage.

"Yes. Like that." Eva's knees gave out. She sat, only vaguely realizing the bed was right behind her, catching her.

Mark followed her down, unhooking her bra as he went.

He held one heavy breast in his hand, rubbing his thumb across her nipple, while he teased the peak of the other with his tongue, making her writhe under him.

Together they lay back, him over her as he kissed and teased and fondled.

Every nerve ending cried out for "More. Please, more. Now, more!"

Mark pushed away from her and stripped off his jeans, grabbing protection from his wallet as he did so.

Eva unzipped her own jeans and lifted her hips while Mark pulled them free.

Then he took up where he'd left off, his mouth tracing the line down her stomach.

When he got to her belly ring, he flicked it with his tongue.

In the back of her mind, Eva realized those high-pitched breathy moans were coming from her.

"More," she managed to say between breaths.

"Say my name," he growled to her.

"Mark," she whispered, knowing why he demanded it of her, more than willing to give it to him.

"Mark," she said again.

"Who do you want?" he demanded.

"You," she gasped. "Only you."

"Now?" He held himself over her, barely touching her, ready to plunge but waiting, waiting.

"Now," she screamed, desire making her world totally centered on the man above her.

And then their worlds collided as they came together, hard and fast and, oh, so filling.

"Mark, Mark, Mark," Eva found herself chanting as they fell into rhythm.

She looked up into his face. It was fierce, strained and totally beautiful.

"Say my name," she demanded.

"Eva." His voice rasped as her fingernails did the same down his back.

Hearing him call her name took her to the place she longed to go—had to go.

"Mark." She screamed his name to the rafters, not caring if the neighbors heard.

"Eva," he responded.

And together they scored a victory beyond their highest expectations.

Mark lay splayed across Eva's bed, one hand cupping a soft, supple breast, the other hanging off the bed.

Her leg lay on his, her hand on his stomach. Overhead, the ceiling fan spun, drying their sweat on their sensitive skin.

He wasn't sure what happened. All he knew was this was so much more than sex.

Which was why he had to go.

He wasn't ready for anything more. Hadn't planned on ever being ready for anything more.

He didn't want to care for Eva, didn't want to know her thoughts, her dreams, her inner driving force. Didn't want to care.

She traced her fingers across his stomach, making his gut tighten as she played him.

Without looking at him, she asked, "Are you okay?"

"Yeah. You?"

"Yeah." She rolled over and off the bed. "What just happened?"

Mark turned his head to look at her, every magnificent inch of her. So much woman. *All his.*

No, not all his. Not his at all. "I'm not sure."

"I've never—not even with— I don't know what to think of this. Do you?"

He braved the intensity of her questioning eyes. "No. Neither do I."

"I know this sounds weird, but it's like I lost myself, then found myself in you. Very metaphysical, I know, but that's the only way I can describe it."

Mark nodded. "That's a good description."

"You don't sound too happy about it. What are you feeling?"

"I don't know what I feel." He rolled off the opposite side of the bed. "I think I need some time. Some space."

"Okay." She pointed to a closed door. "Bathroom through there. I'll be—I'll be in the kitchen, I guess, to give you some privacy."

Privacy. After what they'd done, what they'd shared, privacy sounded like a hard, cold separation of souls.

Mark gave her a bleak look, unreadable beyond unhappy. "Okay. Thanks."

How could such a shared act mean such different things to each of them?

Making love with Mark had been a mistake. Especially because of the love part. She'd gone and done it. She'd fallen in love with a man who didn't love her back.

Was this what Chuck had felt, knowing she couldn't love him as much as he'd loved her?

How could he have lived with the pain?

But, then, he hadn't, had he?

Eva donned the sleep shirt that she'd tossed to the floor earlier, slipped into the bathroom for a second, then scurried out without looking in Mark's direction.

Mark took his time showering, trying to piece together a plan of action, or at least a thought or two about what to do next.

Could he walk away from an experience like this? It had been so surreal, almost out of body.

As hot water sluiced over his head and down his neck and back, he let his mind go, reliving the lovemaking he and Eva had just shared.

Lovemaking. It was too soon for love.

How long did it take to fall in love?

He didn't believe in love at first sight. But, then, he didn't much believe in love at all—even when it climbed into bed with him.

Chemistry. Abstinence. Stress. *Need.* He searched for a reason, for an excuse for what he was feeling.

As he entered the kitchen he found Eva washing his mug over and over again as she stared out the kitchen window into the black night.

She glanced over at him. "Find everything you need?"

No, he didn't even know what he needed, much less where to find it. "Yes, thanks."

"It's okay if you say no. I totally understand." She looked down at the mug as if she was surprised to find it in her hands. "But if you want me to, I might be of some help tomorrow when you go through the process with Aaron."

At her offer, Mark felt like the world wasn't so heavy on his shoulders. So this was what it was like to share the load.

But this was family business and it was up to him to take care of it. He shouldn't burden her with his problems.

"Eva, I..." He paused. Instead of turning down her offer, he found himself saying, "Okay, thanks."

"They'll let Tiffany know when you should show up. Call me when you hear from her, even if it's early."

"I will." Tomorrow didn't sound so daunting with Eva by his side. "Thanks. It's not enough, but, well—thanks."

Her smile was genuine, gentle and very real. "Thanks is plenty."

That smile sustained him all the way home to his empty apartment where he lay on the couch, drifting in and out of sleep, worrying about what tomorrow would bring.

And taking comfort from knowing he wouldn't have to face it alone. Taking pleasure in remembering how Eva had taken away his loneliness. And taking deep breaths as he tried to push away thoughts of an uncertain future.

Eva straightened the covers and climbed into bed. She snuggled down, breathing in the scent of Mark, remembering the feel of Mark, the taste of Mark, and her ecstasy at Mark's skillful hands as they'd made love.

Made love. That meant quite a bit more than *had sex*.

What did Mark mean to her?

She reached deep down into herself, letting the feeling of Mark flow through her. Her body felt satiated, her mind felt rewarded, her heart felt whole.

What did Mark mean to her?

Quite a bit more than she had expected.

What was she going to do about that?

Sleep on it. That was always the advice Chuck had given her.

She snuggled into her pillow. Would he come to her tonight in her dreams, the way he often did?

As she drifted off, her dream lover lay with her, warming her, keeping her safe. When she turned toward her fantasy man, she saw his face.

Mark.

He felt good and right and all hers, in her dreams.

In her sleep, she cried. Her dreams never lasted.

CHAPTER TEN

IF HE HADN'T found tension release in Eva, Mark might have come apart during the night spent worrying and wondering what he could have done to prevent Aaron's predicament.

He tossed and turned, first in bed then on the couch as he flipped through TV channels. He didn't think he'd slept at all.

When Tiffany's call came around eight in the morning, Mark had been up for hours.

"I couldn't get an emergency order for release. They're holding him until Monday when a judge will make a decision."

"That's two days, Tiffany."

"He broke probation. He assaulted an officer. And he has shown no remorse. I've called in every favor I have but I'm still not able to do much here. Visiting hours are at three this afternoon. You can see him then."

As he hung up the phone with Tiffany, Mark resisted the urge to dial Eva's number. Mark hesitated to call. Tiffany had been clear. There was nothing anyone could do for Aaron.

But what about him? Was there anything anyone could do for him?

He found himself driving towards Eva's house, needing her comfort, needing her support. *Needing her love.*

Needing her love? No, he didn't need her love. He was too strong for that.

Still, he couldn't help wondering. Did Eva love him?

Mark thought of the feel of her hands on him as they'd made love. Of the way she'd cried out his name. Of the way she'd clenched around him as if she would never let him go.

Of the way she'd left her imprint on his soul so that hours after they'd made love he could think about her and still feel her brilliant glow inside him.

Sex had never felt like this before.

She came to the door in her sleep shirt, looking tousled and ready to go back to bed.

"Mark?"

"I'm sorry. I shouldn't have…" He stuttered his way through an explanation he didn't have. "I can't see him until this afternoon."

"Come in." She stood aside to let him in.

The buckets of paint in the corner caught his attention.

Would Eva understand? He needed to do something and he needed to do it with her. He'd rather make love, but what if she said no?

He was in no state to take rejection gracefully today. He wasn't sure if he'd ever be able to take it gracefully from her. What had this woman done to him?

"Eva, can we paint? I haven't forgotten you won that game and I owe you."

"Okay." The sympathetic look she gave him told him she *did* understand. She pointed to the kitchen. "Why don't you fix a pot of coffee while I dress?"

Mark rumbled through Eva's kitchen, opening drawers, searching for measuring cups and coffee filters. Instead of feeling intrusive, it felt intimate and possessive. The sense of belonging anchored him.

As they took photos off the walls, Mark studied the people in the pictures. One photo showed a teen girl and two very young children.

Eva looked over his shoulder. "My mom, Ricky and me."

"You look like her."

"Yes, I do. I wish I could remember her." Eva took the photo from him and reverently laid it on the table. "It's the only photo I have of her except for a few school pictures."

"What happened to her?"

"I don't know. She just left one day and has never come back. Our grandmother raised us."

Trust issues. Mark could see where they might have sprung from.

"I'm sorry."

"Don't be. We didn't have a lot of money growing up but we had a loving, stable family. I'm not sure we would have had that if she had stayed."

Mark took another photo off the wall. Her brother and very pregnant sister-in-law, both in their late teens, gazed into each other's eyes, obviously in love with each other. He put it next to the other family portrait. "Love and stability has nothing to do with money."

"What happened with your parents?" Eva didn't look at him as she taped off a window seal. It made answering easier.

"Dad cheated on us." The cold part deep inside him throbbed even after all these years.

"On us? It's very common for children to identify with their parents."

Mark thought about that for a while as he pulled a nail from the wall and patched the hole with toothpaste. "That's how Mom always said it. 'Your father cheated on us.'"

"There are better ways she could have phrased that."

"Neither of my parents are known for trying to make their words less painful." Mark still winced at the blunt way his mother criticized his sister over her few extra pounds. She criticized him over his failed marriage with equal vehemence.

Eva stretched to reach the last picture frame on the wall. "You do pretty well with your diplomacy."

"I have Tiffany to thank for that. She was always telling me how I should say things." Mark had resented the advice at the time, but it had eventually had its benefits.

"Tiffany seems nice." Eva studied the effects of her taping over the wall seams. "This part is done."

Mark covered the last hole. "Done here, too. Ready to paint?"

The primer coat went quickly, with Eva cutting in the trim and Mark rolling.

By the time they were ready for the top coat, the apartment held the kind of silence that called for confession. Mark cleared his throat. Where to begin?

"I wanted a family. Tiffany wanted to concentrate on her career. We drifted apart and she found someone else."

"While you were still married?"

"Yes." Mark rolled paint on the wall with a vengeance. "I wasn't careful with my words when I found out. I acted just like my parents, I guess. She took out her pain in our divorce settlement. It was bitter all round. We're trying to be adult about it now."

As Mark finished up the last of the window seals, he said, "I think I'll clean up now. I only get forty-five minutes with Aaron. I don't want to be late."

"Okay."

He could feel Eva staring at him, evaluating him.

Ask me. Please, ask me if I need you. Ask me if I want you to be with me. If he ever needed synchronicity to work, now was the time. Of course, he could open his mouth and ask her to go with him, but an O'Donnell didn't lean on a woman. He needed some vestige of pride left to stand on.

"Mark, would you like me to go with you? I'll help where I can."

Had she seen his plea in his eyes? Felt it from his heart?

It didn't matter. All that mattered was that he didn't have to face today alone.

Feeling weak, he covered his need by saying nonchalantly, "Sure. Aaron can use all the help he can get."

And so could he.

The look Eva gave him told him she saw through his bravado. "I'll be glad to do whatever I can for Aaron—and for you. All you have to do is ask."

And there lay the difficult part, the asking.

Eva sat in the waiting room with Tiffany, who paced and obsessively checked her phone for emails while waiting for Mark. Eva recognized Tiffany's actions for what they were, a need to do something—anything other than feel helpless.

Type-A personality. Like Mark. She could bet there had been friction in the household of two such like-minded people.

Tiffany stopped pacing and answered her phone with a sharp "Hello." She mouthed the words, "District Attorney" while pointing to her phone.

"Yes, I saw Aaron this morning. The visit went much like last night, except he now has a desperate edge to his bluster. I've counseled him about his attitude, but he's just not getting it."

Tiffany listened intently, a frown marring her forehead. "Yes, we can do that. I know just who to ask."

Tiffany turned to Eva just as Mark entered the waiting room. Whatever she was about to ask would have to wait.

"I've got to get him out of there," Mark told Tiffany as he clasped Eva's hand like a lifeline.

Tiffany nodded. "I'm talking to the District Attorney, trying to work things out. If he would only help himself. Would it hurt for him to be a little remorseful? A little accepting of responsibility for what he did?"

Eva felt Mark's tension through their joined hands.

"He's scared, trying to get through this the best he can. Are you going to do something for him, or do I have to hire another lawyer?" he challenged Tiffany.

Tiffany brushed away Mark's sharpness. "They've done a drug test and we're waiting for the results but they recommend that we get an expert evaluation."

Now Eva knew what Tiffany was going to ask her. Could she do it? For Mark's sake?

Through gritted teeth, Mark said, "He's not doing drugs."

Tiffany glared back at him. "Do you want him out or not?" She turned to Eva. "This is what happened between us."

Caught in the middle of their old hurts, Eva looked anywhere but at Mark or Tiffany. Instead she said, "I'll do it. I need to go by my old office at the clinic and do some research first."

Mark looked like he would protest. Instead, he gave her a half-smile and said, "Thank you. I'll drive you over there."

Eva sat silently, clenching her fists as Mark neared the clinic.

He pulled into a parking place right in front, as though it was waiting for him.

And Eva couldn't move.

But she wasn't gasping for breath, breaking out into a sweat or having a dizzying kind of foggy vision, so she was doing better than the last time she'd tried this.

"Are you okay?"

She hadn't been here since that day—the day Chuck had been gunned down trying to protect her from the drug-crazy kid who had been determined to shoot anyone who moved to get the vengeance he thought he was due.

And she hadn't talked about Chuck's death to anyone out-side the family and her grief counselor. Could she do it? Could she tell Mark of the terror, of the loss and the guilt?

His jaw was set, his eyes bleak.

Not today. She would need his strength to get through the retelling and right now he had none to spare.

"I still can't talk about it."

He gave her a sideways look. "Counseling didn't help?"

"Yes, it did. But I've needed time as well as therapy." She took a deep breath and told him the tip of the iceberg. "I've got post-traumatic stress disorder because of it. That's why I'm out of the field right now."

"Yet you're trying to diagnose my nephew who you've only seen a handful of times—and never in a clinical setting."

To defuse him, she gave him a half-smile. "I've got PTSD. I didn't lose brain cells."

"I'm sorry. I shouldn't have…" He raised his hand toward her, but lowered it again without touching her. "I'm sorry."

"It's okay. I understand you're lashing out. I did enough of it myself when my brother was sentenced to prison. Sticking up for family is like that. But it doesn't help anyone heal."

She rubbed her finger across her lips, remembering. "In fact, it more often tears families apart. My marriage almost didn't make its six-month anniversary. My grandmother said my brother's problems were no reason to leave my husband and wouldn't let me move in with her. Besides, Susan had already moved in with her. Abuelita didn't need a hysterical pregnant teenager *and* a hysterical exhausted medical student invading her tiny two-bedroom, one-bath house."

"It worked out for all of you."

"Not by luck or happenstance. *We* worked it out. Lots of talking. Lots of professional therapy. Ricky is still working out his drug addiction. He'll work it out every day for the rest of his life."

"Aaron's not into drugs. I see drug crises all the time. I'd know if he were."

"You see the patients when they're in crisis. You'd be surprised at how many people appear to be functional in day-to-day society yet they are addicted to legally prescribed, illegal or over-the-counter drugs."

He took his hand off her shoulder and put it back onto the steering wheel. "Do you really think Aaron is into drugs?"

Eva pulled away from him, scooting to lean against her car door.

No subtlety from either of them, just awkwardness.

"I will need to interview him to give you a professional opinion but..."

"But?"

"He's got some signs of anabolic steroid abuse, which won't show up under a standard drug test." She took a breath. "The arresting officers have requested an evaluation for steroid abuse."

Mark narrowed his eyes on her. "That's what you were talking about with them after he was arrested. You told them to check for anabolic steroids, didn't you?"

"They've seen this before, Mark. There's not much those guys haven't seen."

"You didn't answer the question. Evading. I'd expect that from Tiffany, but—"

Eva kept her voice pleasant even under Mark's harsh tone. "They asked for my opinion, purely off the record. I gave it to them for Aaron's sake. Steroids can be very, very dangerous, especially for a developing teen male."

"For Aaron's sake, huh?" He revved up the car. "I'm taking you back home. I think we need to skip this analysis, for Aaron's sake."

* * *

Eva rolled on a thick coat of paint. The last time she'd done this alone, she'd just lost Chuck. Had she now lost Mark as well?

But if she had swallowed her concerns, compromised her principles, would she lose herself?

She painted all day Sunday and through the night until Monday morning, not wanting to go to bed alone.

Her sheets still held the scent of Mark. She could wash them but she didn't want to.

Was love always this complicated?

Love. She was so in love with Mark.

The intensity of her feelings made her sit down hard. Her couch squeaked as she dropped bonelessly onto it.

She hadn't meant for it to happen, hadn't asked for it— hadn't looked for it, like she had with Chuck. This time it had just happened.

The idea of losing Mark was as strong as the memory of losing Chuck. Amazingly, she realized Mark's carried more immediate pain.

For the second night in a row Eva cried herself to sleep.

Eva wasn't sure how he did it, but somehow Mark got Aaron out of juvenile detention and back into school on Monday morning with no one the wiser about his escapade but her.

Escapade. Mark's word, not hers.

She would see him at work, but she'd wanted to get the air cleared before that. She left messages until he finally called her back.

When he called her, his voice held hurt and bewilderment but also a longing that Eva echoed in her own soul.

"I thought we had something together. But I can't turn my back on my family."

"I wouldn't expect you to. But, Mark, ignoring a problem doesn't fix it."

"I wish it could have turned out differently."

"Me, too."

But she couldn't back down on her worries about Aaron, couldn't wave away his symptoms and label his behavior typical teenager because he wasn't typical for a clean teen, but he was very, very typical for a teen steroid abuser.

The boy needed help.

What could she do to make Mark listen?

After a slow, boring night at work followed by a restless sleep, Mark drove toward the studio to get his Friday pre-segment taped. This was not going to be his best day.

What would Eva do? What would she say?

He didn't know any woman alive who could let a break-up go down easily.

Break-up? They hadn't even been together.

But they had. They'd been together in Eva's bed and in his mind. They'd shared a thread that had woven itself deep into his psyche. And breaking that thread felt like breaking his will to live.

With heavy feet Mark trudged towards the studio door, bracing himself to face whatever might come.

As he pulled open the door he swore to himself he would never, ever play where he worked again.

In fact, right now he felt like he would never play again.

He would do it differently if he could. Eva was special and he was certain he'd never find another woman like her. But he had a responsibility to his family. Aaron needed all his time and attention right now, and arguing with Eva about any deeper issues Aaron might have wouldn't help the situation. What choice did he have?

Quietly, he entered the studio. In her white lab coat she looked professional and competent.

The cameras were rolling as Eva gave her spiel.

"If it's a drug, it can be abused. This includes drugs your teen can pick up in the pharmacy section of the grocery store or can purchase online as well as drugs prescribed by doctors and illegal drugs sold by drug dealers.

"Teens are moody by nature so it's hard to recognize behavior changes. Your friends may become alarmed before you do. After all, who among us wants to admit our child is doing drugs?"

Eva looked into the camera. "Here's what you need to know. If your teen is abusing drugs, you need to intervene. It is very unlikely teens will stop abusing drugs on their own. Check your screen for local numbers of clinics that can give you a helping hand."

The camera closed in on Eva. Without flinching, she looked into the lens. "Anyone rich, poor, young or old can be a drug abuser. You can get better. To get better you must ask for help. No one can give it to you until you're ready to receive it."

Offstage, Mark shifted his weight. She'd written this program based on him and his family, hadn't she?

Eva kept talking to the camera. "Asking for help takes great courage. Asking for help isn't a weakness. It's a strength. And you can recover. Everyone here at *Ask the Doc* is pulling for you."

From the floor, Phil said, "That's a wrap. Nice close, Eva."

"Thanks." Her smile was polite but not bright. It held no energy, at least no energy for Mark.

The smile she gave Mark was hopeful and questioning. But he had no hope and he had no answers.

Mark took the script Phil handed him. He would be speaking on the influence professional athletes had over teens. The staff had put together his talking points yesterday, but getting Aaron released and back in school had kept him from running by the studio to pick them up.

He glanced down at them and suddenly felt very manipulated.

His script was on the signs of anabolic steroid use. Paperclipped to the front page was a folded message. From the many scribblings he'd seen in her script margins, he recognized Eva's handwriting.

It read, "My fault. Education is key. I forgot that. Here are the symptoms. Judge for yourself. P.S. I would never, ever deliberately hurt you or your family. I care a great deal for you."

Care a great deal? What did that mean? What did he want it to mean?

He tried to stop the flow of his thoughts but couldn't catch them in time to suppress his desire, his longing, to be loved by Eva.

Love? Where had that come from?

Mark gave himself a smirk. If people knew where love came from, the world wouldn't need poets or musicians.

"Five minutes," Phil said as he walked past him.

As the camera light blinked red, Mark got the cue to read the list.

"'Here are the signs of steroid abuse to watch for in your teen.'" He read starkly and flatly without even attempting to jazz it up or make it interesting.

His gut began to ache even as he tried to rationalize each bullet point as he read them to the camera.

"'Increased oiliness and severe acne, particularly on the back.'"

Most teens had an increase in oiliness and severe acne wasn't that uncommon, especially in humid New Orleans.

"'Rapid weight gain, particularly in muscle.'"

Aaron had put on a lot of weight, particularly muscle

weight, over the summer. He'd even gotten stretch marks on his biceps because they'd increased in size so rapidly. But Mark could easily explain that by the groceries he was always buying and the many workouts he drove Aaron to.

"'Erratic sleep patterns due to type of steroid and use of cycling technique.'"

Aaron's erratic sleep patterns were probably as much Mark's fault as Aaron's. Tiffany had always complained about how Mark's night-shift work had disrupted her sleep, too.

"'Early balding, particularly male-pattern balding.'"

Maybe Aaron's hairline was receding a bit, but that happened sometimes to guys. His dad had thinned out early. It was just the luck of the DNA pool that *he* had a full head of hair.

Mark had to clear his throat before he could read, "'Significant breast size increase in males and shrinkage of testicles.'"

He hadn't really noticed if Aaron's breasts had increased in size and he wouldn't have a reason to notice if his testicles were shrinking. How did parents check for that on their teen sons?

Mark had to clear his throat before he could read, "'Obvious and irrational mood swings.'"

Mood swings hit most pubescent boys, especially when they were having trouble at home like Aaron was. He himself had certainly been a victim of a fluctuating temperament. That's why his coach had made him run all the extra laps at practice.

Making the sign to cut the camera, Mark glared at the stage door Eva had left through. If she thought he was going to suddenly believe Aaron was injecting himself with steroids because of this list she was…

No matter how hard he tried to rationalize it, that gut instinct that served him so well in the E.R. was kicking in.

How did a person start a conversation with a teen about drug abuse?

Mark's glare melted into despair. He could have asked Eva but he'd said too much. Experience had taught him time and time again that once spoken, words couldn't be unsaid.

As he headed down the hallway to change from his suit to his jeans, he looked over at her dressing room.

It was dark and empty. Just like his heart.

CHAPTER ELEVEN

Eva sat in the garden next to her grandmother, holding her hand. Some days, the bad days, touching wasn't allowed but today her *abuelita* didn't seem to mind it.

Because she needed to, Eva talked. She told her grandmother all about Mark's nephew and her suspicions. She explained about Mark's denial and family loyalty. And she talked about how she understood that loyalty because she'd felt the same for her brother.

Finally, she said what had been weighing on her heart most. "I think I love him, Abuelita."

Rare recognition dawned in her grandmother's eyes as she squeezed Eva's hand. "You think you love him? You're not sure?"

Ecstatically, Eva welcomed the gift of lucidity. "I'm not sure he loves me."

Her grandmother's voice was firm, the way Eva remembered it, as she said, "You can't expect him to take the risk of loving you if you don't risk loving him, can you? Love takes trust. You've got to trust him enough to be open with him and to be vulnerable with him."

"But love doesn't mean a person has to back down on her principles, does it?"

"It's not like you to see things in only black and white, Anita. People are made of many shades of gray."

Anita. Her mother's name. Trying not to startle Abuelita
back into her vagueness, Eva said gently, "I want to help him."

Sharpness erased all the confusion from Abuelita's eyes.
"You want to prove yourself. Have you ever made anyone
change his mind by forcing him to agree with you?"

Eva felt properly chastised. "You're right, Abuelita. Trying to force my beliefs onto Mark won't work any better than
it did with Chuck."

Abuelita patted her hand. "Appeal to his mind. Appeal to
his heart." She grinned, her smile crooked, yellow and very,
very dear. "Appeal to his passion. And, Anita, dearest, stop
holding back. I don't mean in bed, I mean in your heart and
in your mind."

Eva flushed and looked away as she thought of Mark in
her bed.

While bed was very, very good, his family came first in
his world. "His passion is his family."

"Whose passion, dear?" Abuelita pulled her hand loose.
"Do I know you?"

And she was gone again, into that murky place Eva
couldn't breach.

During a lull in patients, Mark rested in the doctors' lounge. It
was a cold, lonely place of antiseptic, cracked orange leather-
ette couches and cheap blankets. The TV played an old sit-
com with an annoying laugh track that screeched along his
frayed nerve endings.

What was Aaron doing home, alone, unsupervised? Mark
hadn't wanted to leave him on his own, but he'd had no one
to ask.

Eva's offer to help came to mind.

And so did her insistence that Aaron was injecting himself with anabolic steroids.

He couldn't stop his worry as he thought about the show,

the signs of anabolic steroids and Aaron. And as he thought about Eva.

In the dark of night, Mark let the pain flood through him. How could cutting himself off from Eva hurt so deeply?

He'd let her get under his skin and into his heart and then she'd broken it.

She'd tried to make him choose between her and family.

Family had to be protected.

Mark stopped himself right there. When had his father ever protected family?

How many nights had he lain in bed while his parents had fought downstairs? She'd been drinking. He'd been sleeping around.

And Mark had been told not to tell. What would the neighbors think? Maybe it was family *secrets* that needed to be protected?

As the frigid air crept beneath his thin blanket to wrap around his throat, he remembered Eva's bed. Eva's body. Eva's heart.

She had a good heart. A caring and sincere heart.

Yet she'd advised the police to test Aaron for drugs.

Why would she do that?

The truth rang through.

Because it was the right thing for Aaron.

Not because she wanted to expose family secrets to add to society's rumor mill. Eva cared nothing for society.

She cared for people. She cared for Aaron.

And once upon a time she'd cared for him.

But once upon a time only happened in fairy-tales and he had proved he was a real frog without a drop of princely blood in him.

But, then, Eva was no delicate princess who needed a white-knight rescuer either.

And in the real world real people had a chance to talk

things out—at least he hoped they did. Personally, he'd never tried it.

He dialed Eva's number, getting her voicemail message.

"You're right. Aaron might be doing steroids. All the signs are there. I'm sorry." The words weren't as hard to say as he'd thought they might be. But then he had to swallow hard to get the rest of it out. "I need your help."

He hung up, waiting for the world to crash around him, for his father to tell him how weak he was and to be a man, for his mother to dissolve into hysterical tears, for him to feel two inches tall.

And none of that happened.

Instead, his phone rang.

Eva.

"Of course I'll help." She took an audible breath. "I need your help, too."

He'd picked up Eva as soon as his shift was over. Now, as the sun came up, Mark sat outside the substance-abuse clinic, waiting as she fought her internal battles.

He would wait forever for her. Now that they were "back together" he could breathe again.

He had almost lost her. Almost lost himself.

Because he'd refused to let her in.

Now he finally understood what Tiffany had been saying all those years.

Tiffany had wanted him to let her see inside him, to connect, even to share his burdens.

But he hadn't let her. His father had never let his mother. Men shouldered the load. Women rode on their backs.

Because if a woman ever stood on her own two feet, she could realize she could walk away.

It's what his mother had finally done.

It's what Tiffany had finally done.

It's what the O'Donnell men practically forced their women to do.

He wouldn't make the same mistake twice.

Beside him, Eva did her own thinking. Alone, when she could be leaning on him. But he wouldn't rush her. He would be there for her when she was ready for him.

"Eva, how can I help?"

Eva twisted her non-existent ring on her finger. Her face was pale, her eyes shadowed. She drew in a ragged breath then let it out again in a burst.

"I haven't been back to the clinic since—since that day. I need to tell you about it. I need you to help me face my fears."

"Do you know how much I care for you? How much I…" Mark looked away then back again. "I would do anything for you, Eva."

"I do more than care for you, Mark." She opened the car door and slid out to stand on the sidewalk.

More than cared for him. Could that mean she loved him?

When Mark could think well enough to open his own car door, he joined her as fast as he could.

Before he could say anything, she grabbed his hand. "It started here."

"We had a gang member in with his girlfriend. She'd gotten into something hallucinogenic and we were trying to get her inside the building. I was talking to her, trying to bring her back to enough reality to get her to sit in a wheelchair. She thought it was an electric chair and kept screaming that she didn't want to die like her daddy had."

Mark put his arm around her waist and she leaned into him.

"Then another car pulled up. Three boys climbed out. Their colors showed they were with a rival gang." Her eyes were unfocused as she pulled him along the sidewalk toward the front door. "Apparently, one of them had been the one to sell her the drugs. He thought she had ratted him out to the police. But she was too incoherent to say her own name correctly, much less anyone else's."

Eva's shoulders slumped under the massive pain she carried. Mark wanted to take that load from her, carry it himself for her if he had to. Anything to keep her from hurting. But all he could do was be there for her.

"And then what happened?" he asked, to pull her back to the present.

"I was talking to them." She turned to him. The look in her eyes begged him to listen, to understand. "I'm trained to do that, you know?"

Mark nodded, giving her the validation she seemed to need so badly.

She studied him for three heartbeats before she blinked and released him from her gaze.

"They were about to leave. I'd convinced them to go."

Eva pulled him toward the clinic, stopping two feet from the door. "Someone had called the police, of course. This was Chuck's beat, so he was the first on the scene."

"I told him to back off. I told him I was handling it." Rage fought with grief on Eva's face. "Half a dozen squad cars came screaming round the corner, spooking all of us."

"The leader pointed his cellphone at me, yelling that I'd set him up. So Chuck challenged the leader, drawing attention away from me. Someone yelled something about a gun."

"And there were guns. Gang members, police, everybody had guns."

Her voice broke. "They shot Chuck."

She started crying hysterically as she sank to the concrete and Mark sank with her. He held her as she fell apart, shaking, sobbing, railing at the world.

Through her crying she told him about the other members being shot down by the police, about the girl breaking free and running into the line of fire, about her guilt and grief and loss.

And about her anger. If Chuck had only trusted her, he would be alive now.

Trust.

So easy to say. So hard to do.

Finally, she cried herself out. Meekly, she let Mark lead her back to the car.

Mark didn't know what he'd have done in Chuck's place. Most likely the same thing Chuck had done, he thought.

Mark drove her home and walked her to the door.

"Come in. Stay."

He would never tell her no. He didn't think he could even if he had wanted to.

Gently, she rubbed the circles under his eyes. "You need to sleep."

Mark understood what Eva was doing. She was in her caretaker role. It was her identity and she needed to exert it.

He caught her hand and kissed her fingertips. "Only if you hold me."

She smiled through her tear stains. "I can do that."

She led him into her bedroom and unbuttoned his shirt.

In his ear, she whispered, "Take them off," while she ran her finger inside the waistband of his jeans.

He obliged, kicking off his socks and shoes and reaching into his wallet for protection while she peeled off her own clothes.

"Would you like to lie down?" Eva waved her hand to indicate the bed.

"Okay." He lay back while she took the lead. Mark had always taken the lead, never given up control. But this was all for Eva and whatever she wanted he would give to her.

She moved his arms up above his head so he was stretched across her bed. Starting at his wrists, inch by inch, she ran her fingers over him until every nerve ending cried out for release.

Mark clenched and unclenched his fists, wanting to touch, wanting to feel Eva's smooth skin. But this was her game and today she made the rules.

Minutes, hours, days. The world spun around them as they became the center of the solar system.

"So strong. So mine," Eva said.

"So yours," Mark confirmed.

He reached out to her, ran a finger across her nipple and watched her shudder. The satisfaction that he could affect her so deeply sat well within his core.

Then she straddled him.

He ran his hands down her back, feeling the shape of her curves under his palms.

And together they proved to the universe how much they were right for each other.

Eva dozed, waking to stroke the outline of a biceps or to entangle ankles, then drift off to sleep again. Sleeping naked next to Mark was the most comfortable she'd ever been in her own skin.

When a cellphone rang, Eva thought it might be the television station. She'd called and left a message after she'd spoken to Mark, saying she would meet them onsite that afternoon since they were all caught up with studio work.

But it wasn't her phone. It was Mark's.

At first he didn't take the call. But the phone rang repeatedly, the caller obviously not content to leave a message.

Eva watched his expression turn from concerned to disbelieving to resigned.

"Those are the consequences, Aaron. I stand by your coaches' decision. I'll pick you up after school."

When he hung up the phone, he explained to Eva, "Aaron

was bragging to some friends about being arrested again. His coach kicked him off the football team. He's too prideful to ride the bus. No other senior does. I should probably make him. Humility would do him good. But I want to talk to him so I've got to pick him up." He grabbed his jeans and shirt and headed to the bathroom.

Eva joined him, washing his back and wishing she could do more. "Next time," she promised him.

"Next time. I like the sound of that."

Eva hesitated. *Take risks.* "Would you like me to come with you?"

At first Mark looked like he would brush her off. But then the tension eased a fraction around his eyes as he said, "Yes. Absolutely. I can definitely use your skills."

Before they even arrived at the school, one of the coaches was already calling back. Aaron was in the football locker room, holding the water boy hostage.

Of course, they were calling the police.

Mark edged up his speed and made it to the high school in record time. They even beat the squad cars.

Once at the high school Mark and Eva went directly to the locker room.

Inside, in the back behind the rows and rows of lockers, Aaron had the boy in a head lock.

"Aaron, I'm coming in."

"Okay."

"I'm bringing Dr. Veracruz with me."

Aaron stayed silent.

Eva called back to him. "I can help, Aaron. Give me a chance."

Barely audibly, he answered, "Okay."

As Mark listened to the caller, Eva watched. Once they cleared the lockers, Aaron stopped them ten yards from him. "Don't come any closer."

He tightened his grip on the boy, making his hostage squirm.

Mark was about to charge the two of them until Eva put a restraining hand on his arm. "We won't come any closer until you feel okay about it, Aaron. Loosen your hold a little, okay?"

He must have because the boy stopped wiggling and began gulping in air.

"I really messed up this time, didn't I, Uncle Mark?"

What should he say? Mark looked to Eva.

Eva read his look and stepped forward. "Hi, Aaron."

"Hey, Doc."

"Why don't you let go of the kid? He's not looking too happy there."

"If I do, what will happen to me?"

"Not as much as if you don't let him go." Eva took a cautious step forward. When Mark would have followed her, she held up her hand. "Why don't you hang back, Uncle Mark, and give Aaron some space?"

Giving Aaron space was very important. He didn't need to feel trapped, especially with that young boy under his control like that. He was irrational. No one could predict what he might do.

Mark took a step back. "Sure. Whatever you need, Aaron."

"What I need is to play football. And I need Sharona back from that place her parents made her go to."

Eva took the conversation away from such an inflammatory topic. "You're not feeling so great, are you, Aaron? Feeling a bit anxious? Maybe a little ungrounded?"

She nodded, encouraging Aaron to nod back.

"Maybe a little," he agreed.

She could feel the tension roll off Mark at her back. If she could, so could Aaron. Yet he was the most stable person in Aaron's life. She had to keep them separate but visible. If she could get to Aaron, maybe he would respond to human touch. If he was anything like his uncle, she knew he'd had too little of it in his life and would respond well to it.

Eva took another step forward. "We can help you."

He shook his head. "Nobody can help me." His voice was anguished, tortured.

"I can." She gave him a grin she wasn't feeling. "I've got connections."

"What kind of connections?"

"I know a place where you can get your head together. You can be safe and everyone around you can be safe."

Aaron gave her a suspicious glare. "Where's that? Jail?"

"You need help, Aaron. You've been taking steroids, haven't you?"

"Yeah, but they're not like drugs. They just make you bigger."

"They also mess with your head."

"I don't want to stop."

Eva nodded. "I understand. We can talk about that when you let the boy go."

Aaron tightened his hold on the boy, wringing a squeal from him as his face turned red.

Outside, she heard the wail of sirens.

For a second her past came back to her. Chuck. The girl. The gangs.

But then she blinked and saw only reality, two very scared boys. One of them could cause great harm if not handled well.

With the sirens closing in, Eva needed to do something fast or this could end very badly. "Trade him for me."

Before anyone could protest, she made quick strides to Aaron and put her hand on the thick arm that could too easily strangle the boy. With the other hand she rubbed his back in slow, soothing, circular motions.

He didn't pull away. Instead, he leaned into her ministrations. Through Aaron's shirt she could feel the tension in his back.

"Let him go, please." She didn't dare look at Mark.

But Aaron was staring at him. "What am I going to do, Uncle Mark?"

"Aaron—" Mark's tone was menacing "—let the boy go."

Eva sent Mark a warning look. "Uncle Mark is going to back off now. He's going to run outside and tell everyone you and I are coming out. Right, Mark?"

Mark sent her a fierce frown. When he hesitated an ugly fear started to coil low in her stomach.

"Please, Mark. Trust me."

He gave a single nod and made a quick exit.

"Now, Aaron, while it's just the three of us, let's make it only the two of us. Easier all round, okay?" She gave his arm a pat. "You can put your arm around me if you'd like. But I promise, even if you don't, I won't leave you here alone."

When Aaron hesitated, she went with her instinct and hugged him. "I'm so sorry your mom's not here for you. But I'll take care of you. I'm very good at taking care of teenagers."

"You promise?"

How many broken promises had Aaron been fed in his life? Yet he still held hope.

Which gave her hope for him.

"I promise, Aaron."

"Uncle Mark trusts you." His eyes darted to where Mark had been standing.

"Yes, he does." She kept up her slow, methodical backrub, feeling the tension ease the slightest bit.

"Okay, then."

Aaron loosened his grip on the boy, who ran as fast as he could out of the locker room.

Eva caught Aaron's hand in hers. "That's a good start. Now we can make some progress."

"How? How can we make progress? I saw the police cars through that window."

Eva didn't need to feel the tightness in Aaron's back to know they'd just taken a step backwards in this situation. She heard it in the cracking of his voice and saw it in the wildness of his eyes.

"I hadn't seen the window, Aaron. There are several police cars out there, aren't there?" Blue and red light flashed from the bar lights on the tops of the cars. Another element to alarm the unstable teen. How was she going to get them both out of there unharmed? "Let's come up with a plan, so the police won't be worried about us. We want to stay calm to keep them calm, okay?"

"Okay." Aaron's shirt became drenched in sweat as his central nervous system went crazy. He punched himself in the head, a blow that would have dazed an average-sized kid. "I can't think of any plan."

Eva gave him another hug, trying to keep him settled. "It's okay. I have a plan. Ready to hear it?"

This time Aaron shrugged free. "Tell me." His tone was turning belligerent as he was beginning to despair.

She moved her hand to his arm, the lightest of touches with no hint of restraint. "Here's what we're going to do. I'm going to hold your hand and walk in front of you. Stay close to me. When we get outside they're going to want you to drop to the ground. Do that immediately, okay? I'll stay right next to you."

"Then what?"

"Then they'll cuff you. I'll tell them you need medical attention. They'll put you into a squad car and take you to the hospital. Your uncle and I will be right behind the squad car and will follow you in. I'll talk to a couple of doctors I know and then we'll start getting you better, okay?"

"Okay." Now he sounded like a meek little child.

Eva caught Aaron's hand. "Let's do it."

Obediently, he followed behind her, staying so close she could feel his body heat against her back.

Mark stood just outside the door, where he had obviously been listening. How had he managed to make it back with all the police outside? She would ask him later.

And there would be a later for all of them.

She gave him a tight smile. "Good! You're back!"

"I'm sorry, Uncle Mark. About everything. If this doesn't work out, tell Momma I love her, okay?"

Eva cut him off to keep him focused. "We'll talk about that later. Right now, Uncle Mark is going to walk right behind us. Stay very, very close to Aaron, Mark. Put your hands on Aaron's shoulders."

"Will do."

"Now, Aaron, put your hands on my arms." Those massive hands would be too close to her throat if he put them on her shoulders. The police wouldn't like that.

Eva had to admit she wouldn't like it either.

"Ready?"

"Ready," Mark answered from behind her.

With Aaron's recent past, she couldn't predict the kind of action the police might feel they needed to take.

Aaron gripped her arms a little too hard.

"It's okay to be scared. Everyone gets scared, don't they, Uncle Mark?"

"Yes, they do." Mark cleared his throat. "And we all need help sometimes. Remember that, Aaron."

"I will, Uncle Mark."

Carefully, they walked in sync out of the gym.

Everything happened exactly like Eva had said it would—which was nothing short of a miracle.

As three policemen scrambled to cuff Aaron, Eva slipped her hand into Mark's. "We'll do everything we can to do what's right for him."

Mark held himself together until they loaded Aaron into the patrol car. The boy was streaked with dirt. He had muddy tear tracks down his cheeks.

It was the tears that broke Mark.

He wrapped his arms around himself, trying to find the strength to follow the squad car.

Then Eva wrapped her arms around him, too.

"It's okay to cry," she said as tears coursed down her own cheeks. His emotions made her love him all the more.

Mark nodded, his throat too thick to answer.

Eva drove while Mark ruminated on all he could have done, all he should have done, to prevent this.

She left him to his own thoughts as she drove to the hospital.

Once there, they checked in on Aaron through the glass. Handcuffed to the hospital bed, he already looked more settled in his mind at the restraints.

"That happens fairly often," Eva explained to Mark. "Patients who were out of control often calm down when they no longer have to be responsible for their own actions."

"He was such a cute, funny little kid." Beside her, Mark reached for her hand. "Thank you for being by my side. I felt so helpless. So lost. Having you next to me gives me the strength I need to hold it all together. I couldn't do what I need to do for Aaron without you here with me, helping me keep my head on straight."

Through the wired glass he stared at the nephew he had failed.

As if Eva could read his mind, she said, "It's not your fault. Aaron made bad choices."

"I thought I was paying attention. But I didn't even see the signs after you pointed them out."

"Mark, as private as you are, you're not going to like this, but it would help if you talked to someone. A professional counselor can help you through this."

"You?"

"Not me. I'm too close to you."

"Too close." He searched her eyes. "How close?"

"This isn't the most romantic time or place, but I mean this in good times and in bad ones." Eva caught his hands. "I love you, Mark."

I love you. That felt so—so full. So big. So much like the piece that had been missing from him all these years.

The words were out before he could stop them. "I love you, too."

Then, because it felt so good, he said it again. "I love you, Eva Veracruz."

She grinned at him. "That's Dr. Eva Veracruz to you."

"So where do we go from here?" Mark realized this was the most important question he'd ever asked.

Eva, being the take-charge woman he loved, had her answer ready. "After we get Aaron settled, we talk about marriage."

"Will that talk include babies?" Mark could almost see a dark, curly-haired daughter or two to spoil.

Eva kissed his cheek. "Yes. Babies and families and boundaries."

"Families that bind but don't strangle, right?"

"Our families?" She arched a brow in mock surprise. "I have a feeling they'll do a little of both. But that's what we have each other for. So we can find and keep our balance, right?"

"Right." Mark hugged Eva, needing some balance right now. "I love you, Eva Veracruz. In good times and in bad."

EPILOGUE

EVA COULDN'T HAVE asked for a better wedding day. Her brother stood ready to walk her down the aisle to a beaming Mark, who looked so handsome in his dark suit.

On the balcony, a saxophone sang of joy and triumph of the soul.

She had opted to skip the traditional tux, knowing her brother could ill afford to rent one. Instead, Ricky looked very handsome in the jacket and tie he'd bought for his daughters' christenings.

"You look nice." He kissed her on the cheek.

"You, too."

"That's what Susan said." He waggled his eyebrows at her. "That's why we were late."

His two youngest daughters, dressed in leotards and tutus they'd picked out themselves, strained on either hand of their big sister as Selma, Eva's junior maid of honor, led them down the aisle. Halfway down they decided to show off their cartwheel skills, despite their big sister's best efforts to stop them.

They weren't the best-behaved flower girls in the world but they were the cutest.

Selma looked very grown up in her first long dress and long white gloves like the debutantes wore.

Eva had themed it a fantasy wedding. Her family had followed orders and dressed accordingly.

Behind them, Susan, her matron of honor, wearing a sparkling halter dress that would have looked lovely in a ballroom, pushed Abuelita's wheelchair in front of her.

Abuelita wore a tiara on her head. Selma had insisted she would like it. It seemed Selma was right. Abuelita kept forgetting whose wedding she was attending, but she was fully aware that she was center stage. Halfway down the aisle, she began waving to friends in the pews as if she were the Queen Mother herself.

Her family might not be dressed according to wedding etiquette but they thought they were beautiful. Eva agreed.

Since she'd missed her cue, Ricky tugged on the sleeve of her red silk dress, the one she'd been wearing when she'd first met Mark. "Your turn."

"My turn," she agreed.

Ricky would be doing double duty, acting as her escort then standing next to Mark as his sole groomsman.

It was an unconventional wedding procession but, then, they were an unconventional family.

More traditionally attired, Mark's mother and her husband sat in the first pew. His sister and her newest boyfriend finished out the aisle, with Aaron between them. They had all been co-operating so well in their family counseling sessions that Aaron had received a day pass for the wedding.

Behind them sat Mark's father, his wife and Mark's three half-siblings, all in their mid-teens. It looked as if Mark's dad had learned something about parenting since he'd left Mark's mom.

Better late than never, Mark had graciously said.

The television station's camera crew filmed the whole thing. It was her goodbye present.

While she and Mark had boosted the ratings, she'd turned in her resignation letter, anyway.

Unlike Mark, Eva wouldn't even try to double-dip at two jobs at once. She didn't have the type-A driving temperament.

Besides, they soon wouldn't have much time on their hands outside the nursery.

Her gut instinct had prompted her to pee on the stick this morning. Definitely pregnant.

Tonight, she would tell him about the baby.

Mark watched Eva walk towards him in her scarlet dress. Was it possible she was showing even more cleavage than the first time she'd worn it?

As she stood across from him, he couldn't stop staring, drinking her in, glorying in her becoming his wife.

She leaned forward and whispered, "I don't think the society mavens approve."

Mark leaned forward and whispered back, "It doesn't matter what they think. I approve." He stared down at her cleavage. "I very definitely approve."

Ricky bumped him with his elbow. "Do that later. Right now, say your vows."

Mark took Eva's hand, loving that frisson of energy that shot up his arm. Loving that he would have the benefit of her special touch the rest of his life.

"I, Mark Chandler O'Donnell, take you, Eva Anita Veracruz, to be my lawful wedded wife *and the mother of my child.*"

He loved the shocked surprise in her eyes. She followed it up with that brilliant smile of hers.

He was in for a rocky ride as a protective parent if he had a daughter with her mother's smile.

Afterward, at their reception, he took great pleasure in lifting his glass to their guests.

"May I present my family?" A feeling of contentedness

filled him as he swept his glass around the table to include all Eva's and his relatives.

His family had been broken and hurting and he hadn't known how to heal it. But his wife, the doctor, had known exactly what to prescribe.

And he intended to spend the rest of his life thanking her for it.

Love. It truly was the best medicine.

"To your health and the health of your family!" he toasted his guests.

Eva leaned over and clinked her glass of sparkling water to his champagne flute. "To our family."

* * * * *

A sneaky peek at next month…

Medical Romance™

CAPTIVATING MEDICAL DRAMA—WITH HEART

My wish list for next month's titles…

In stores from 5th July 2013:

❑ Dr Dark and Far-Too Delicious – Carol Marinelli

& Secrets of a Career Girl – Carol Marinelli

❑ The Gift of a Child – Sue MacKay

& How to Resist a Heartbreaker – Louisa George

❑ A Date with the Ice Princess – Kate Hardy

& The Rebel Who Loved Her – Jennifer Taylor

Available at WHSmith, Tesco, Asda, Eason, Amazon and Apple

Just can't wait?

Visit us Online

You can buy our books online a month before they hit the shops! **www.millsandboon.co.uk**

0613/03

MILLS & BOON
Book Club

Join the Mills & Boon Book Club

Want to read more **Medical** books?
We're offering you **2 more** absolutely **FREE!**

We'll also treat you to these fabulous extras:

- Exclusive offers and much more!
- FREE home delivery
- FREE books and gifts with our special rewards scheme

Get your free books now!

visit www.millsandboon.co.uk/bookclub
or call Customer Relations on 020 8288 2888

The World of Mills & Boon®

There's a Mills & Boon® series that's perfect for you. We publish ten series and, with new titles every month, you never have to wait long for your favourite to come along.

Blaze
Scorching hot, sexy reads
4 new stories every month

By Request
Relive the romance with the best of the best
9 new stories every month

Cherish
Romance to melt the heart every time
12 new stories every month

Desire
Passionate and dramatic love stories
8 new stories every month

Mills & Boon® Online

Discover more romance at
www.millsandboon.co.uk

- 🌹 **FREE** online reads

- 🌹 **Books** up to one
  month before shops

- 🌹 **Browse our books**
  before you buy

...and much more!

For exclusive competitions and instant updates:

 Like us on **facebook.com/millsandboon**

 Follow us on **twitter.com/millsandboon**

 Join us on **community.millsandboon.co.uk**

Visit us Online   Sign up for our FREE eNewsletter at
www.millsandboon.co.uk